Andrew Madsen Smith

Luck of a wandering Dane

Andrew Madsen Smith

Luck of a wandering Dane

ISBN/EAN: 9783337196608

Printed in Europe, USA, Canada, Australia, Japan

Cover: Foto ©Andreas Hilbeck / pixelio.de

More available books at **www.hansebooks.com**

LUCK

OF A

WANDERING DANE.

BY

HANS LYKKEJÆGER.

PRICE, 25 Cents.

FOR SALE BY ALL NEWSDEALERS.

CONTENTS.

LUCK

OF A

WANDERING

DANE

BY

HANS LYKKEJÆGER.

[Native of Denmark, Citizen of the United States.]

Soldier and Sailor, Moulder and Merchant, Tramp and Trader, Soap-boiler and Scribe, Peddler and Philosopher, Overseer and Understrapper, Jack-of-all-trades and Master of Fortune.

Dedicated to
NOBODY,
For the Benefit of
EVERYBODY.

PUBLISHER'S ADDRESS,
P. O. Box 754,
PHILADELPHIA,
PA.

MATLACK & HARVEY, PRINTERS, 224-28 S. FIFTH ST., PHILA.

INTRODUCTORY.

(WHICH IT WILL BE WELL TO READ, THOUGH IT MAY BE "SKIPPED.")

I write and publish this *True History of the Early Portion of My Life*, because it pleases me so to do.

What moral the reader finds in it, is supplied gratis, and can be applied at pleasure.

I believe that the story of every man's life, for thirty years, conveys lessons and warnings of value to his fellow creatures.

I adopt a *nom de plume;* in certain cases the names of persons and localities are changed in order to prevent identification and there all fiction ends.

All the adventures, mishaps, incidents and details, set down in this book are the true, actual experiences of the single individual who narrates them.

I am sure that, after reading my story, no one will charge me with a desire to glorify, or make myself appear a better man than I am, or to cover up my sins.

The strange vicissitudes of my life *might* have crowded upon any other man, I only tell *my* story and believe that it proves that "Truth is stranger than Fiction."

There is much herein recorded that I tell with sorrow; but I determined when starting this work to tell the truth and I have adhered to that resolution even when it laid bare my most serious offences. I have, in later years, earnestly tried to do my duty in every particular, to make what amends I could for former sins. I have not to look to man for forgiveness and remission.

I have attempted no elegance of style, have copied no man's literary peculiarities in my work; that the story will prove interesting, if only from its strange and varied incidents I am certain; of its absolute truth I am anxious to convince by renewed assurance.

.I am, very respectfully,

The Public's obedient servant,

HANS LYKKEJÆGER.

LUCK
OF A WANDERING DANE.

BY

HANS LYKKEJÆGER.

[Native of Denmark, Citizen of the United States.]
Soldier and Sailor, Moulder and Merchant, Tramp and Trader, Soap-boiler
and Scribe, Peddler and Philosopher, Overseer and Understrapper,
Jack of all-trades and Master of Fortune.
Dedicated to
NOBODY
For the Benefit of
EVERYBODY.

CHAPTER I.

MY FATHER AND MY MOTHER AND MYSELF.

That I was born, I am prepared to present positive *prima facie* proof
in about 250 *lbs.* avoidupois, of what I sometimes, in summer, consider
much "too solid flesh."

For the benefit of those who may, after reading these pages, desire to
make a pilgrimage to the scene of my nativity, and for the information of
future historians, I state with the utmost precision of date and detail, that
I came into this world of vanity and vexation of spirit, in the cottage of
my father, situated in the town of Knusböl, Parish of Jaarop; near King
river, eight miles from Kolding Castle, close by the battle ground of Queen
Margaret, in Juteland, Kingdom of Denmark; hour, 8 A.M.; day, Thurs-
day; date, February 4th; year, 1841.

I hear individuals of the present time, who are inclined to slang, say,
"It is a cold day when I get left." It certainly was a very cold day
"when I got left," for the first time in the welcoming arms of my happy
mother. The howling winter winds were whistling and the snow flakes
falling thick and fast about the humble home of my parents, and the storm
had been raging for days. When my father was called upon to sally forth
for the assistance always deemed necessary, if available, upon such critical
occasions, he found the doors and windows so blocked by the snow drifts
that he was forced to make his exit up and through the chimney, and to
struggle almost as hard for his life outside as I fought and gasped for my
own within.

I do not state these facts, or events immediately subsequent, from personal observations made by myself at the time; the information is derived
from my mother, who was present throughout the entire proceedings, and
I have no reason to doubt the reliability of the record.

In fact, I was more a dead baby than a live one, and for the first few days of my existence my battle for life against adverse physical circumstances was fully as hard as the fight for a living proved in after years. I was a poor inanimate chunk of mortality, without voice sufficient to pipe a greeting for the anxious mother's ears, or strength sufficient to strike out, after the manner of most babies, with wild, red lumps of fists and feet, as though striving to swim in and against the "sea of troubles" into which I had been pitched; and the religious belief of my parents causing them to consider baptism necessary to salvation, the minister was summoned at almost the same moment as the midwife, that my safety in the next world might be insured providing I took a hasty departure therefor. Whether it was the christening ceremony or some wise woman decoction turned the scale in favor of my remaining upon this planet, I cannot say, but,—I didn't die.

My father was a blacksmith, the prize son of Vulcan in that section of his country. Nature had been in a most liberal mood, when she distribu-

ted the materials for his manufacture and his brawny bulk was distributed over six feet, two inches of longitude. Upon an equally lavish scale of anatomical architecture was my good mother erected, and she, after the old fashioned manner of wives in those days and regions, gave willing, steady and valuable aid at the forge and all craft work, to my smith-father. If I inherited nothing else from my immediate progenitors, the great, robust body which has withstood many rough buffettings, and the solid, sound head, even though it be somewhat thick, which has forced its way through heavy opposition, are endowments which have proved more valuable to me than coin and land, and for which I have learned to hold them in grateful remembrance.

Once I had grappled a hold on existence, I grew strong and lusty, and in a few months was able to prove that my lungs were in primest of working order and my voice possessed of as much power as it had not sweetness; and swaddled, in a modified form, not unlike an Indian

THE BIG SMITH.

pappoose, as is the custom of the country, in bandages that prevented all action of my lower limbs, I made up in vocal exercise for the constraint placed upon my well rounded legs.

When I was two years of age my father died, and with four children, I being the youngest, to provide garments and grub for, my mother was forced to exert her strength, mental and physical, to the utmost. She endeavored, for a time, to continue the blacksmithing trade as before, which her expertness in the craft rendered her perfectly competent to do, but to meet all demands at the forge and give the necessary attention to the many wants of such a family of noisy, mischievous youngters, was entirely too great a task even for her ; she disposed of the workshop and its implements and removed to her native town Nyborg.

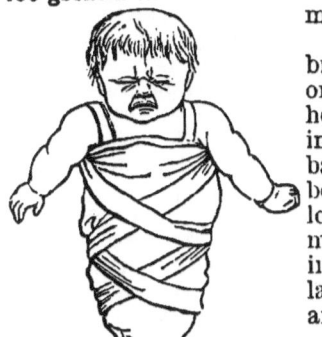

In the place of her birth my mother started bravely to earn a livelihood for herself and little ones by peddling fish. No light or easy work was hers; buying the scaly commodity from boats, in the town, she placed them in an immense basket which was strapped upon her back and, bearing her heavy burden over rough roads and long miles, through wind or storm, cold or heat, mud or dust, she tramped into and through the interior country, trading the fish for produce, ladened with which she would return to the town and there convert her barter into cash.

This is the way my Danish mother toiled for and supported her children; hard work never

YOURS TRULY.

dampened her spirit, subdued her courage, or dulled her keen woman's wit, and in 1848, during the Danish-Prussian War, when my brave little

mother-country held its own and "conquered a peace" with the powerful invaders, her business aptitude developed itself and she secured a contract to supply food, and cook for, one thousand soldiers, and with such wisdom and system did she conduct her business, that after fulfilling every obligation to the satisfaction of all concerned, the settlement of accounts left a balance on the right side of the books, which amounted to a considerable fortune in that country and raised her considerably in the social scale.

Blessed with a competence which secured her from want, my mother, though never idle, for, as the saying is, "there was not a lazy bone in her body," did not return to the laborious fish and produce packing. She speculated in a quiet way, in goods and property, and continually increased her store. Although she was at that time a buxom, healthy beauty of a woman, I feel sure, speaking from the light gained by my mature experience, that every additional hundred dollars added in her bank book, heightened her attractions and decreased the number of her years in the estimation of mankind; at all events the wealthy widow had plenty of suitors for her hand (and what would be in it). That blind

MOTHER.

little villain, Paddy Cupid, prosecutes his archery practice in Denmark with the same disregard of fitness and common sense which marks his indiscriminate shooting and hitting all the world over ; he managed to get astride of my good, big mother's handsome nose and blinded the eyes of her understanding with his soft wings, until she finally accepted, for better or worse, one of his recruits as successor to my father. As is too often the case, her choice proved decidedly "for the worse;" a good-looking, dashing fellow of a spendthrift took possession of the widow, family and fortune. It required but twelve months' time for him to squander the hard earnings that three years of weary toil had accumulated; then he left us and after a time my mother procured a divorce, though every now and again he would make his appearance, poor and penitent, destitute and dolorous, and make his peace until he had re-filled and refitted, when he would again take himself off until necessity obliged him to repeat the performance. This continued for seven years, when he died from the effects of dissipation.

The year 1850 found my mother sadly impoverished from the cause mentioned; with characteristic energy she applied herself to the task of re-building her fortune; but the scene of her past prosperity had become distasteful to her and she removed to near Gram, in Schlesvie, where, in a roadside inn, to which was attached a few acres of ground, she devoted herself to the cultivation of business and crops with her usual vigor and moderate success.

At this place I was entered at and supposed to attend the country school. I was nearly ten years of age and such a solid "chunk of a boy," that Stumpy, Shorty, Fatty, and like impertinent references to my personal appearance and peculiarities, were the names by which I was commonly saluted, much to my disgust. My attendance at school and my habits of study were decidedly irregular, and though I contrived in some way to pick up the rudiments of knowledge: the three R's, "'readin', 'ritin' and 'rith-metic," yet the actual manner of such acquisition is a mystery which I cannot even at this time explain.

An attempt to educate me while at Nyborg had most signally failed, for at that place the institutions of learning were still in use as military hospitals; soldiers and men-of-wars-men were as yet numerous about the

SCHOOL HOURS.

fortifications and in the harbor, and days and hours, when I should have been gathering wisdom at the school desk, I passed among the wearers of uniforms and blue jackets who varied the monotony of their life by making of me a pet, errand boy, foot ball and shuttle cock. One of my favorite amusements was to slide down or be dragged down the glassy slope of the fort, a performance productive of such disastrous results to the rear section of my breeches that my mother, tired of the incessant patching with cloth, re-seated, or half-soled, the seat of my garment with leather, and thus furnished material for an additional offensive nick-name to my persecutors.

Dealing in potations and digging potatoes soon proved too monotonous for one of such active temperament as my mother, so she disposed of her business and property, moving once more, this time to Apenrade, a town celebrated for ship building, where she opened a small hotel, accommodating citizens with board, lodgings and refreshments.

CHAPTER II.

I BIND AND UNBIND MYSELF.

"Why don't you put him to work?" said one.

"He ought to be learning a trade!" said twenty.

"Make that big, lazy cub earn his bread!" said a hundred.

"That boy will be ruined if he don't get a master!" said everybody.

Such was the burden of the song that was sounded in my mother's ears, day and night, by all the innumerable choir of friends, acquaintances and gossips that, in Apenrade, as in all other places, were very willing to attend to the business, and arrange all matters for everybody but themselves.

I had almost reached the age of fourteen years, and was certainly big enough, old enough, and ugly enough, to begin to scratch gravel and hunt worms for myself. I was not lazy or unwilling to work, but I was slow and could not at once conclude what trade, business or profession I would honor by devoting to it my abilities and life. I was, maybe, like the man who said that he "must have a great deal of mind, it took him so long to make it up."

However, my mother's and my own opinion at length began to run on a line with the oft and gratis expressed advice of outside friends and busybodies, and after due consideration, I notified and horrified my mother by announcing my desire and intention to be a doctor, and requested her to furnish me the necessary funds and opportunity for study.

"A doctor!" cried she, with hands uplifted at my presumption, "a pretty doctor you would make! And where do you suppose the money is to come from to pay for making you a doctor?".

"I supposed you had it, and would give it to me," answered I.

"You did, did you?" she replied; "when you do, for a wonder, get an idea into that thick skull of yours, why don't you try to get a sensible one there?"

"Well, I want to be a doctor, anyhow," I persisted; "if you can't give me the money, that's the end of it."

"Suppose I could and would give you the money, how am I to give you the brains, you donner-head! Do you think I have a supply of brains in the drawer, or the bank, or put away in a stocking to hand out to you like bits of money ? No, no, my lad, you'll be no doctor with my consent or making. I don't want it on my conscience, or to have you hung for poisoning any fool of a patient that would take medicine of your ordering. No doctor for you, sir, choose a trade."

Finally, understanding that I must abandon all hope of learning the medical profession, I was, by my own choice, apprenticed to learn moulding in an iron foundry. Why I selected that particular trade I cannot tell, unless it were from some vague mental connection between burying the patterns as a moulder, and doing the same for patients as a doctor ; but go to the iron foundry I did though I had no decided inclination for that or any other craft work. Nature never intended me for mechanical production. I can fully appreciate, understand, apply and manage machinery, but to build it or any portion of it, I am unfit.

I did not apply myself very diligently to mastering the mysteries of the moulder's art, and even had I been disposed and eager to learn, the opportunity was not afforded me in the place to which I was apprenticed. I was at the foundry all day, no eight or ten hour law there or then, and attended school at night, but my "business" hours were employed with malt instead of mould, intoxicants in place of iron.

Boy's boy was I, a beer-burdened beast, a brandy-wein jug-jerking jackass. At beck and call, whistle, nod, or gentle hint (such as a tool or other missile thrown at my head), of every other employee of the works, I had to seize the empty beer or rum mug, can, jug or bottle, and rush to the tavern to have them filled, returning and delivering them to some of my multitude of masters only to start off again on the same errand for others.

My excursions back and forth were many, repeated and continuous; my efforts to please, I own, were not incited either by love of the work or those who imposed it upon me, and I did not always, or even occasionally, afford entire satisfaction to my task masters; but my pay was prompt, very; and plenty, exceeding and over-plenteous; though it was in a coin I neither coveted or demanded, in fact would willingly dispensed with; it was the remuneration generally given a young bear, "more kicks than half-pence," curses and hard names being thrown in with reckless extravagance.

"Stupid!"—"Fool!"—"Lazy Brute!"—and pet names of like character were showered upon me with a liberality only exceeded by the bestowal of the kicks, cuffs and blows which were rained down with unstudied impartiality, which could be reached by the foot, fist or missile of the petty tyrants whose unhappy slave I was.

Forty men were always employed at this foundry and the hands were constantly changing, and for two years I was compelled to be the recipient of all the malicious and cruel persecutions which hundreds of brutalized natures could invent or learn one from the other, and to suffer all the tortures that drunken barbarity could inflict upon a defenceless object.

Two years I remained at this place and during that entire time I did not see a single employee in the foundry who was not addicted to over-indulgence in intoxicating liquors. The pay of a journeyman moulder, then and there, was about seventy-five cents per day; at piece work he could earn a dollar in the same time; boarding was but $1.25 per week and other necessaries in proportion. Beer could be purchased for what was equivalent to two cents of American money, a quart; I would mention however, in order to prevent a possible migration of an army of beer lovers to Denmark, on account of the low figure above quoted, that prices have

LEARNING MY TRADE.

raised since the time of which I write, and through Bismarkian taxation that seductive beverage averages there in cost as much as it does in the land of the Star Spangled Banner.

Moulding in a foundry, in those days of Denmark, was considered the best paid mechanic's work in the kingdom, yet, through intemperance and improvidence, such was the poverty of these moulders, whose wages, wisely used, would have enabled them to live in comfort; that among the unmarried men it was common to make one decent coat serve three or four —one of the party, arrayed in the presentable garment, being the only representative of the lot who could appear at the Club meeting or in public on Sunday, the other partners having to keep in close quarters and shirt sleeves or their old rags until their turn arrived to use the good coat.

For the first twelve months of my apprenticeship, I was paid at the rate of fourteen cents a day, out of which sum I was obliged to furnish my own food and clothing; my income was certainly not calculated to lead me into riotous living, but trifling as was the amonnt I have seen many days, after my arrival at man's estate, when I would gladly have toiled hard all day for even that sum. My wages were increased to twenty cents per day for the second year, and would have been advanced at the rate of ten cents per diem for each of my remaining years of apprenticeship until at the end of my five years' servitude, I would have been receiving three dollars per week.

But two years of misery, constant abuse and heart-sickness, caused by the besotted condition of those by whom I was every and all day surrounded, so disgusted me with the life I was leading that I resolved to cut loose from it and all its belongings. In my heart and head, even though the one was considered as particularly sluggish and the other as being unusually thick, I had, born within me, or unknowingly acquired, thoughts and feelings which caused me to shrink from my then contact, and though I had been called "stupid fool" and considered as such, until I almost concluded I was one, I determined that I would not sink to the brutal level of those about me. I felt an ambition stirring within me to prove that the wisdom of the fool was better than the folly of those who considered themselves as wise men, and I mustered all of that quality which in me, then, was called obstinacy, pig-headedness and other choice names of contempt, the same characteristics which, in a youth more fortunately situated, or of higher social standing, would be dignified as firmness, courage, etc., I gathered together all of this that was in my nature, and proceeded to interview and astonish my master.

When I approached the proprietor of the foundry, and quietly but decidedly asked that I might see my articles of apprenticeship, the man's face would have answered as a picture of Balaam's when that ancient individual's donkey addressed words of wisdom to him.

"Wha! wha! wha-t!" he spluttered, "what's that you say?"

I repeated my request.

"Want to see your contract! Would like to look over your articles! You fool! You ass! You double-doubled dunder head! What do you mean?"

"I want to see," said I, "if in my articles of apprenticeship there was put anything that made me to be a slave to all the drunken workmen in your foundry, and to take all the kicks and blows they saw fit to give me; that's what I mean."

"Oh! that's it, is it; only that. Well, I'll soon show you," roared the old head tyrant, and with the curses, coming thick and fast, he kept time with his fists upon my unlucky head and body, continuing his lively illustration of what it was my duty to be, to do, and to suffer, until my anger and indignation got the better of discipline and subordination and I determined that the game should not be all on one side.

He was a great, powerful man, but I was a good sized, stout boy, and had not received so many hard knocks without learning how to give back some of the same in return; so at last I struck out boldly in my own behalf, and fought with a desperate determination which, added to his surprise at my resistance, rendered it no easy matter for him to handle me, and there was the liveliest kind of a fight, in which the victory of course was on the side of the strongest, but when we were separated, and that only through the intervention of his big wife, who clawed my face and gathered handfuls of my hair ; he had plenty of bruises to rub, and pains to groan over, as well as myself.

EXPLAINING MY INDENTURES.

There was a terrible tempest in the family tea-pot when I went, battered and tattered, home to my mother and reported that I neither could or would remain longer at the foundry and submit to such treatment as I had for two years endured.   Here was rebellion indeed ; the traditions of the land, laws of the country, society and family were all outraged by this "donner headed fool" who had impudence to insist that being kicked, cuffed and cursed, with the continual carrying of rum and beer for human brutes, would not learn him the trade of moulding, and could not be considered as part and portion of a regular apprenticeship.

My mother, good, sensible woman though she was, had the old fashioned ideas regarding as obligatory the perfect submission in mind and body, of the servant to the master.   To spare the blow, she thought, was to spoil the boy, and she could understand no other system.   Consolation for the curses showered upon me by the irate master she gave me in a torrent of Danish "jawing," and though I am certain that she had never heard of the homœpathic theory that "like cures like," her remedy for the bruises under which I was smarting, was a liberal application of a stout, strong broom-stick, with which she whacked me until she was tired, and I was worse sore than ever and I roared for quarter.

"You've broke my back!" I howled, as I rubbed and squirmed.

"You've broke my heart!" gasped she, gathering her breath and undecided whether to give me another dose of the broom handle, or to have a good cry for her own relief.

"I've been father and mother to you; I've toiled and slaved to bring you up," she cried, and her words were true; "and you've disgraced yourself and me, and all your family, and you're trying to ruin yourself and kill me."

I protested that I had no intention of doing either.

"You will go back to your master and beg his pardon, and ask him not to put you in jail as he could and ought to, and beg him to take you back and promise to obey him in all things. That's what you will do at once."

"I won't!" said I.

"You will!" said she, and grabbed again for the broomstick.

"I won't!" said I, taking care at the same time to keep out of reach of the weapon.

"I won't!" I yelled, as I shot out of the door.

And I did'nt go back.

Every time I ventured near my mother, for days after my retirement from trade, I received her positive orders to report and submit to my old master, but I stuck to my determination not to do so, and again the tongues of the old gossips wagged in prophecies of my final and ignominious fate. I not only was "a fool, a natural born fool," they said, but I was also an abandoned ruffian of the most desperate character, who had assaulted and nearly killed my master and his wife, two perfect creatures, in amiability and generosity akin to angels. That I would certainly be hung, provided I didn't starve to death through laziness, before the time came for killing me with a rope, every one of these old croakers was fully convinced.

At last my mother realized that under no compulsion would I return to the foundry, and began to consult me as to my future movements. I informed her that I had made up my mind to go to sea, and then there was another scene of reproaches, objections and refusals on her part, and stormy, stolid obstinacy on mine. Constant droppings, however, wear away a stone, and my continual reiteration that I would go to sea finally broke down her determination never to consent to such a step, and she unwillingly gave me her permission to try the life of a sailor.

To get to the sea required that I should find a captain willing to receive me on board his ship, and though that town then turned out more sailor boys than any other port in Denmark, my big, clumsy body and well-known reputation as a stupid, stubborn, unmanageable cub, did not cause the skippers of the harbor to show extra anxiety to secure my valuable services and my efforts to obtain a place on any kind of a craft were unavailing, though I hunted and applied most industriously.

Nothing daunted by the ill-success of my applications to the unappreciative captains of my home port, I concluded that what could not be done

15

there might be effected elsewhere, so with my mother's tears, kisses and blessing, I started off to find a ship and fortune. My available cash consisted of two Danish dollars, my wardrobe was bundled in a pocket-handkerchief, and was light as my heart the morning I bid "good-bye" to my sole parent and started off for Copenhagen.

My mother had given me her consent and nothing else, this was through no unkindness on her part. She thought that if I had not the means for an extended stay in a strange city, and did not succeed in finding a place on a vessel, I would quickly return to my home and be satisfied to remain there, but in order to insure my comfort, she privately furnished the captain with whom I took passage, a considerable sum of money to be supplied me, if necessary, to keep me from want; all this, however, I did not know at the time.

Half of my cash, one dollar, I paid for my passage upon a sloop bound for Copenhagen, and on August 27th, 1857, I turned my back upon my home to fight the battle of life in the big world, for myself.

OFF TO SEA.

CHAPTER III.

A LIFE ON THE OCEAN WAVE.

I was fully aware that the dollar remaining of my cash capital would not long support me in Copenhagen and idleness. Health, strength and willingness to work I possessed, and grappling the first that offered, I for days after my arrival, earned my bread by the sweat of my brow, as a laborer on the wharves of the city, trying continually in every spare moment to obtain a place on a vessel.

I had too much pride or mulishness, to write to my mother, telling her of my ill-success and asking for money to keep me there or enable me to return home. Had I known of the provision she had, in her kind thoughtfulness, made for me, I might have applied to the captain of the sloop for the money she had placed in his hands and have made use of it, but as I was in ignorance of her action, I stuck to the heavy labor I had secured and grinned and bore it. Go back home, I determined I would not.

The fact that I had never been to sea, my clumsy, overgrown appearance, and the absence of a pass or permit from the authorities of my home town, without which no one in Denmark can enter into any legitimate business or avocation elsewhere, all combined to prevent me from securing the employment I desired, and it was ten days or more before I received the precious and necessary document from Apenrade. With this official guarantee that I was not a criminal or runaway, and license to work, started once more, with renewed hope and vigor, in search of a chance "to plough the roaring main."

How to reef, haul and steer I knew as little of, as I did of tight rope dancing or Greek, but I was not particular regarding the rank in which I entered the marine service, and when at last I found the skipper of a Holland schooner, "Albertino," who was not prejudiced against me by my unpromising exterior, and who offered me twelve Danish dollars (equal to six of the same named American coin) a month, to go as cook upon his vessel, I jumped at the situation, and considered myself a made man.

I was ignorant of cooking as of navigation, and was honest enough to confess the same to the captain, but that worthy man, not having the fear of a terrible death by dyspepsia, or poison before his eyes, consoled me by informing me that with patience and perseverance and instruction, inculcated through the medium of freely given and frequent "lickings," I should soon graduate a most accomplished and scientific *chef d'cuisine*.

Though my experience of meat and potatoes was confined entirely to devouring them when, properly prepared, they were placed before me, and all I knew about coffee was to gulp it down from a cup, yet I tackled the mysteries of the cook's galley with a hearty good will ; the patience and perseverance were stock in my nature and the "lickings" had been such a large element in my past life and labor that I considered them a most necessary and inevitable accompaniment of any subordinate position, so the promised liberality in that particular was no very disturbing influence in my mind, as my back, indeed, my whole body had become almost insensible to any commonly powerful blows. Familiarity in this, as in other matters, was productive of contempt.

It was on a Sunday morning when I first assumed my new dignity and officiated as high priest of the cook's galley. I was told to put the pot on the fire preparatory to making soup ; I so did. I ventured, likewise to fill the pot with water, and after it commenced to boil I felt that I was making headway rapidly. That the meat and vegetables furnished me were, somehow, to be put in the pot and finally resolved into soup for the stomachs of the hungry sailors, I was also aware, but the manner of such introduction and combination was an unsolved problem in my mind. But I boldly plunged the fruits of the earth into the pot and they boiled, and boiled, and boiled, until about 11 o'clock, when, thinking I had better not trust too much to luck, I reported progress to the captain.

"The vegetables are in the pot, sir, and have been boiling hard for about two hours. Can I now put in the meat ? "

The captain could speak no Danish, but as I was able to jabber a little of the low German, or Holland Dutch, and to understand it fairly, I was able to communicate with him.

His reply to this my first official communication and application for instruction, he delegated to the mate, and that worthy proceeded at once to initiate me into the secrets of soup manufacture through the medium of a rope end, with which he forcibly and strikingly illustrated the accompanying lecture, until I was rescued by the kindly interposition of the captain's wife, who good naturedly took upon herself my work for that day, while I served as pupil and dishwasher, much to the satisfaction of myself and the crew, an eatable dinner being enjoyed in consequence, which it would most certainly not have been had its preparation depended upon my efforts.

The next day was "Bean-day," and when the materials were furnished me, my instructress gave me careful directions as to their cooking, the captain and mate supplementing her lesson by informing me that if any or all of the beans were burned, all the calcined were to be eaten by me, and that it would be their duty, which they'd certainly not neglect, to see that I did so devour them. I regret to record that, not only upon the occasion of which I write, but upon many subsequent, I was forced to feed upon burnt beans to an extent far beyond my appetite and my natural receptive capacity, and in consequence of such enforced surfeit in that particular article of diet, I utterly loath the sight, smell and taste of beans to this day. That Heaven had provided their food, and that their cook had been sent from an exactly opposite locality, was the frequent and publicly expressed opinion of all the honest mariners upon the Albertino for many a day after I had entered upon my duties as ship's cook.

We sailed in ballast from Copenhagen for Hermngsand, Sweden, to load with lumber. On entering the Baltic Sea, I first experienced the agonies of that terrible malady, sea-sickness; under its depressing influence, if I was worthless as a cook before, I was worth nothing as anything after it had once taken a grip upon me. I was a useless cumberer of the deck, and to get rid, so far as possible, of my body and bulk, they dumped me down into the hold amongst the ballast, to all of which I was totally indifferent, my only feeling being fear I might have to live some hours more in agony. It seemed to me that I "throwed up" each and every portion of my internal economy, and I would have cheerfully "throwed up" my prized position as ship's cook, and walked ashore, had such a proceeding been possible.

After "affliction sore long time I bore," by advice of some of the

crew, I adopted the regular nautical remedy, simple but effective, which consisted of a piece of fat pork attached to the end of a stout cord; the greasy morsel is swallowed, and then hauled up through the channel it descended to the surface. Three or four operations of this forcastle stomach-pump polished off any crumbs remaining in my well evacuated interior, and after about twenty-four hours of solitary misery upon the ballast, I was allowed to transport, as best I could, all that was left of me to my bunk; once there, appetite quickly asserted its demands, recovery quickly followed, and I never again suffered from sea-sickness. This course of treatment is not, so far as I know, laid down in any regular medical work, or prescribed by the faculty, but I can bear witness to its prompt and

JACK'S PRESCRIPTION.

thorough results and bestow the receipt upon mankind gratuitously. Preparing or spoiling food was not the only duty or occupation of my life. On board the vessel was the captain and two mates, three seamen, the captain's wife and myself ; as I shall refer to some of these again, I take the trouble to give the census. When not busy in the cook's galley, I found plenty of other employment ; it was my duty to keep clean the captain's cabin, and the forecastle where the sailors bunked, and the table service of the crew devolved entirely upon me. As the "ship's boy" I had also, in fine weather, to attend to and "make" gallant and jib sails, the only light canvas we carried ; our vessel being brigantine rigged. If I failed to "shin up" the ratlines with that celerity which my anxious preceptor, the mate, seemed to think it was necessary for me to exhibit in justice to his careful training, my movements were hastened by the quickening caresses of that ever handy rope's end, and with it he soon spurred my ambition and bodily movements into agile expertness.

One bright remembrance I have of those early days, was the constant kindness shown me by the captain's wife, and her influence exerted, in my behalf, saved me many interviews with the rope's end, which through ignorance or mischief I fully deserved. She was as good and bold a sailor as ever trod a ship's deck, and a skilful navigator, having spent her life in a Galliot on the North Sea. In stormy weather she would dress in the oiled overhauls and other "duds" of the sailor, as is common among the Holland women who follow the sea, and would go aloft to furl or reef sail with any man on board ; there was not a detail of the ship's working that she was not able to perform or superintend. She was a good woman.

CHAPTER IV.

TO BRAZIL AND RETURN.

In the six weeks occupied by our trip to Sweden, I learned the ropes, to handle the sheets, to take my turn at the wheel, and to prepare the food sufficiently well to suit the not over fastidious appetites of the sailors, and I considered my apprenticeship ended in that profession.

On our return to Copenhagen, I was agreeably surprised to find that my mother was so far reconciled to my new venture in life as to send me a trunk containing an abundant outfit of clothing, boots, shoes and all necessary articles for comfort. I had written her from Sweden, and I found this very acceptable evidence of her affection awaiting my arrival.

Dressed out in my new clothes, I waited upon my captain and notified him that I now intended to abandon the pots and pans of the cook's galley, to rate myself as A 1, able seaman, to quit his vessel and service and to ship as full sailor with another skipper. The honest king of the quarter deck once more brought the ponderous guns of his philosophy to bear upon the light earthworks of my resolution. He shifted his cud, closed one eye, looked me all over, opened his mouth, and spoke these words of wisdom.

"Look here, lad, don't you go and be a fool all the time, grip on to a little common sense once in awhile. You've learned to 'tend sheets, to cook grub as well as eat it, to steer, and to take such lickin's as is good for your health and necessary for your education. Well, then, now you're calculating to desert your ship and me, as has been a father to you, and to go into another ship, where you will have to learn the ways of new men, and get acquainted with a fresh rope's end as you ain't used to, and a mate's fist as you don't know the knockin' down power of, and a lot of other misfortunes too numerous to mention."

"Don't you be a fool, don't for just this once ; I'm bound for Marvin, Brazil, this voyage; content yourself with friends as is like brothers to you and come with me to Brazil, where there's all the good things of earth to be had for the pickin, and beauties of yaller gals by the hundred. Don't you go and be a fool now, and chuck away a chance for to sail in company with all the blessin's you've been so lucky as to tumble against, dont you do it."

His argumentative artillery was too much for me, and I signed articles to remain with him.

There were but few incidents worthy of record during our voyage to South America, but of those few there is one I will never forget ; it was in connection with a game of "hide and seek," in which the crew indulged when near "The Line."

One of the crew was a Norwegian who had gained my friendship and confidence by many little acts which showed unusual consideration for my greenness, and I trusted him implicitly. This man pretended to make a bet with the rest of the crew, that he could hide me where they would never find me. At his direction I ensconsed myself in an empty barrel which he covered over with heavy canvas, and on the top of this he placed many articles of heavy weight. I was crowded down in these close quarters, nearly suffocated but still chuckling gleefully over our success, as I heard them running about, making pretence of looking for me, when— dash ! splash ! souse !—half a hogshead of sea water came pouring into my nest and I came scrambling out, with eyes, nostrils and mouth filled with the briny element, spluttering like a drowned rat.

Never doubting my friend when he sympathized with me and proposed another trial, I consented. He then instructed me to throw a rope over the bow of the vessel, first making it fast inside, and then to clamber down and hang at the end of the line until our shipmates acknowledged that they could not find me. The preparations were speedily made, and in a few moments I was dangling a few feet above the waves, exulting over the success of our scheme, when the rope was suddenly cast loose from above, and I found myself struggling in the ocean, while the row of grinning faces over the ship's side showed that I had been "sold again." I was soon drawn up on deck, and through policy, joined in the laugh raised at my expense.

I resolved, however, that the practical jokes should not all be played upon one victim, and I studiously watched for opportunity to repay my tormentors in kind. By telling tales to a Dane about what two Norwegians said of him, and then reversing the order to the others, I soon stirred up an intense antagonism between the parties, which resulted in a terrific triangular fight in which all were well mauled. But when the battle was over, and explanations ensued, my part in the disturbance or agency in originating it was made manifest, and all three turned upon me and administered such a forcible lecture upon tale bearing and lying, that its impression made my bones ache for a week after.

The result of my first attempt to obtain what I considered would be satisfaction for the tricks played upon me, only made me thirst more

greedily for further revenge and I contrived to get even, in my opinion,
with one of the Norway men by working upon his superstitious fears. He
was a firm believer in ghosts and stood in deadly horror of them. Obtaining a sheet from the captain's bed, I secreted myself behind some of the
deck lumber during his night watch, and in the gloom and silence of the
quiet, dim hours, I arose before him, enveloped in spectral white, and as

NORWAY'S GHOST.

with a long stick I extended the sheet far above my head, I gave vent to
the most dismal, unearthly groans I could utter. The fright of the man
was terrible, his demoralization complete, and he aroused the ship's crew
with the violence of his shrieks. While the others were quieting him and
listening to his explanations, I slipped away, returned the sheet, crept into
my bunk and was to all appearances in deep slumber on the return of the
crew, who cursed me for a sleepy-head who could not be wakened by
Gabriel's trumpet unless he hit me over the "knob" with it.

My inclination and ability to sleep on all proper and improper occasions, and my indulgence in extra naps was a source of constant annoyance to my shipmates and myself; as I had to cook early and late in each day, lend a hand at the ropes and sails whenever required, and stand my regular watch at night, I could not catch up with my broken rest, so I would "drop off" at all times and in all places about the ship, to be rudely awakened by a can of coffee slops dashed into my face, or a drenching bath from buckets of sea water flung over me. The dose was always active in producing immediate results, but a lasting cure could never be effected.

Of course I was forced to undergo the regular initiation inflicted upon all greenhorns on their first crossing the Equatorial Line. Old Father Neptune made his visit to our ship as usual, with due ceremonies and observances. The representative of the ocean deity came on deck from over the side, armed with a trident, his head crowned and covered with long locks of white flax. Seated in due state upon the throne prepared for him and surrounded by his attendants, he commanded that I should be brought before him to render the homage due from a novice. I was so brought.

His majesty, after a short catechism regarding my name, nationality and sundry impertinent and personal questions, proceeded to have me put "through a course of sprouts" of the most extended and severe nature. I was thrown over the side of the vessel and baptized by being dragged through the sea by a rope, then I was hauled, hand over hand, all breathless and waterlogged, up and on board, where I was lathered over face and head, in eyes, mouth and nostrils, with filthy tar, after which my face was *shaved* (scraped raw) with a section of an old iron hoop serving for a razor, a process which only served to force still further into my skin, and there fix beyond power of soap and water to remove, the vile compound with which I had been plastered. It took the work of days, the hardest of scrubbings and the renewal of several coatings of my skin before I was able to

BAPTIZED BY NEPTUNE.

entirely eradicate the ill-scented evidences of Father Nep's attentions. I can hardly believe it now that I was so "jolly green" in those days, that I then and for weeks after fully believed in the reality of the old Sea King. His appearance on and disappearance from the deck were so managed that I could see nothing of the means thereof, and all preparations for the masquerade had been carefully hidden from me.

Our voyage to Brazil lasted eleven weeks, and just before arriving at Marvin we were boarded by a pilot who was a black man; he was the first negro I had ever seen, and as great a curiosity and subject of astonishment to me as had been the ocean monarch under whose treatment I still smarted.

Throughout the return trip my blunders or ill luck continued, and even increased, and my life was a series of misfortunes, accidents and continual misery. On one occasion I was called from the cook's galley to serve in my other capacity as sailor, and sent to fix something at the top-gallant tree ; the work required more time than I had anticipated, and a pot of beans, intended for dinner of the crew that day, which I had not removed from the fire, by neglect or want of power to attend to, I found rendered utterly uneatable. I discovered this disastrous state of affairs on my return to the galley from aloft, and before anyone else had detected it. I at once overhauled my inventive faculties for some way in which to shift the blame and inevitable punishment from my own to other shoulders. Now we had a very lively pig on board who lived in a pen on the deck, though now and then he would find his way out of confinement and enjoy a little run before re-capture.

Puzzling my wits how to save my own bacon, I happened to think of piggy, and I resolved in an instant to upset the pot, spill the contents, turn the pig out of the pen, and into the beans, and then blame the poor porker with the whole transaction.

My brilliant conception I at once carried into execution, the pot was overturned, the beans scattered over the deck, the scape-goat turned loose and into the mess, and the whole play seemed a complete success.

But my unlucky star was shining brightly over my head and exposed my ill-deeds, for the old captain, through a little spy hole in his cabin, had witnessed the entire transaction. He said nothing, however, until I had gone to him and reported, with well feigned horror, the terrible deeds of the pig, and when I had delivered my sad and well prepared story, I was confronted with the truth, emphatically informed that my word was unreliable, plainer terms being used; and given also to understand was I that my mind and back could be prepared for the reception of twenty-five lashes, well laid on. The skipper remarked that he knew he had the right pig by the ear that time.

It was in vain I prayed to be forgiven and spared the lashes ; the captain said he was willing to forgive me, but he also insisted upon giving me the lashes. He was sure I needed them as a moral corrective, and they would do me good; I offered to do without them or bestow them upon any one else, but the fatherly instincts of my commander and his religious sense of duty would not permit him to recall his orders, and the twenty-five lashes were laid on—well laid on—by the unsparing hand of the robust mate, and then with sore heart and back, I was required to prepare another dinner for all hands excepting myself. I was forced to share the mess I had made with the pig and make my in-

23

terior the stowage place of a hugh lot of burnt beans and dirt, the feast winding up with the promise of a dainty dessert of twenty-five more lashes, even more heartily laid on, by the refreshed second officer, than the original quarter hundred.

Accustomed though I was to having my digestion aided by muscular tonics, the first serving up was rather too rich for my stomach, and the pain and excitement caused me to be in a terribly nervous condition. After the crew had done their dinner, as I was washing out the pot in which it had been cooked, and before I had received the last portion of my reward of demerit, I was summoned to prepare my back for its delivery. At that moment I was holding the unlucky pot over the side emptying out of it the rinsings. The call to the foot of the mast so agitated me, that, in a frenzy of terror the iron vessel slipped from my hands, and in a second had disappeared beneath the waves. Utter despair took possession of my entire being, and I cast myself into the ocean after it, determined to end a life that seemed a never ceasing round of misery.

HYDROPATHIC CURE FOR SORROWS.

The cold contact of the water quickly changed my desire to escape trouble by that means, and on coming to the surface I gladly availed myself of the bouyant assistance of an empty chicken coop the captain threw over as a life preserver, and after that eagerly clutched a rope and allowed myself to be picked up by the jolly boat and conveyed on deck, where the healthy circulation of my blood was restored and insured by the immediate application of the lashes promised, with a few extra to make sure of the count ; there was nothing mean about my captain or his mate in serving out such luxuries; and I was then told that if I still felt any inclination for cold water, as a cure for my bruises and sorrows I had official permission to jump overboard at once, but that no more chicken coops would be wasted on me.

I didn't jump.

CHAPTER V.
MORE TROUBLE AFLOAT AND ASHORE.

My unfortunate experiences on board this ship were by no means ended, though the return voyage was drawing to a close when the trouble narrated in the foregoing chapter occurred.

One day I was employed with others in hammering rust off the anchor chains, when one of the party said to me:

"Cook, go to the mate, will you, and ask him for a pair of goggles to keep these rust chips out of my eyes."

I felt miserable and wanted friends and sympathy, and so was inclined to be obliging, but as I started on the errand, my Norwegian friend notified me that this was another sailor's catch, and that I should certainly catch the rope's end if I went to the mate with the request. This new attempt to make me get more thrashing made me savage, and as we would be in port in about two weeks' time, and as I was heartily tired of the never ending blows the second officer dealt out to me, I at once determined to take that opportunity to pay him a portion of what I considered I owed him. Accordingly I secreted a stout, hard piece of rope in my shirt bosom and then went boldly up and requested a pair of goggles.

"Goggles! goggles! you lubber, I'll goggle you!" and then I found that my shipmates had not misinformed me of the reception awaiting my application. The rope's end of the mate at once commenced to play upon my body with its usual briskness, but the surprise of the tyrant was far greater than that intended for me when he found that I had the twin to his weapon, and was using it upon his head and hide in a way that showed an earnest intention, even if it lacked the brilliant and artistic execution of his more practised hand.

A QUESTION OF EYE GOGGLES.

Mr. Mate did not take kindly to his own medicine, and the ropes were soon dropped in order to bring fists into play, and a pugilistic encounter, not scientific, but very energetic, raged fast and furious until I finally succeeded in getting my antagonist down upon the deck, and I was "polishing him off" in a way that seemed likely to settle all outstanding debts between us and pay him something in advance, when I was pulled off by the captain and crew.

Of course this violent argument did not tend to make my position or life any more pleasant during the remainder of my time on that vessel, but it convinced the bullies that I could and had made up my mind that I would take my own part, and gained for me that respect which is accorded to every man who shows that he is willing to fight for his rights and defend himsef from abuse; my back received far fewer visitations from its intimate, but not valued, acquaintance after that turn up.

At last we arrived in London, England, where the cargo we brought from Brazil was to be delivered, and I was a happy man, or boy, when I received my discharge papers and pay.

FIRED OUT.

I found myself in that great metropolis, my own master and the proud possessor of a fortune of ten pounds sterling, a sum which seemed to me inexhaustable wealth, an opinion that was unpleasantly dissipated after a short acquaintance with and experience of the land sharks who feed on poor Jack.

Considering it my duty to see all that was to be seen, I started out in search of information, adventure and entertainment, first, however, paying out half of my cash for a dandy sailor rig that was worth just about one-eighth of the sum it cost me.

After roaming and gaping about the city all day, I fell in with, as was my usual luck, one of the most tender hearted, disinterested, and benevolent of individuals, who earned his honest living by combining the advocations of landlord and shipping master, and with this good Samaritan I engaged board and lodgings for two shillings a day. The interest this amiable philanthropist took in my welfare was intense, overpowering ; he was unwilling to leave me out of his sight, that I should ship in a vessel where my wonderful ability would be properly appreciated and rewarded he insisted was to be his particular care, consequently he objected to every captain I spoke of going with, and continued his more than fatherly supervision and advice until I had not a penny of my wages left, and was indebted to him for a week's board.

Then he " fired me out " into the street.

The change in sentiment and action of my late friend left me in a most unenviable predicament ; penniless, homeless, a stranger in a strange land,

A'PEALING FOR GRUB.

without employment or food, and unable to ask so as to be understood for either. It was in vain I wandered, day after day, about the docks and made application on ship after ship; no captain wanted me, no Englishman would hire me.

Now and then I would, by signs, strike up a casual acquaintance with a good-natured, lazy, or boozy cook on some of the ships I boarded, and then I would be given a chance to fill up with a square meal in return for peeling potatoes or doing scullion's work about the galley. Most days, I starved.

My lodgings were large and airy, requiring no door key, being the streets or arches under the railway piers or brewery vaults. My dandy rig was rapidly becoming as well ventilated as my places of repose. With empty stomach and pockets I tramped day and night through that immense city, searching for some way in which to earn a crust, and finding it not.

Though to save my life I would not deliberately plan and execute a robbery, yet on one occasion, in the recklessness of mad despair I participated in a transaction that cannot be called honest or even be excused under the plea of dire necessity.

With several other sailors, all equally "hard up" or "low down" as myself, I was wandering disconsolately through the London streets, all more than half starved; I know that, for three days I had not eaten but a few crusts of dry bread. The attention of three famished, destitute men was arrested by the delicious smell of cooking food arising from a basement refreshment establishment, which advertised its viands by displaying upon shelves on the outer side of the door, several rows of pies.

How our empty stomachs did yearn towards those pies, as they stood in tempting array, seeming to call "come and eat me," to the passer-by. Hunger silenced all moral sense; some of those pies we resolved to become possessors of, and a conspiracy was at once formed to secure the coveted food.

NO PA(I)NES SPARED IN DOING A PI(E)OUS DEED.

An arrangement was soon made; as usual all risk and injury was parcled out as my share of the details, and in foolish good nature promptly accepted by me as a perfectly natural result of any division of labor. The plan of operations, that I was to be shoved violently down the steps and against the door, as though assaulted by unknown men, while my companions grabbed and made off with as many pies as possible, was immediately carried into effect.

The assaulting party so realistically executed their share of the drama that, instead of being thrown against the bottom of the door, I was shot directly through the glass that formed the upper half, causing confusion enough throughout the shop for them to complete their part of the programme and covering me with cuts and contusions in a manner that I considered totally unnecessary and over sufficient for the proper enactment of my role.

I lay half stunned and bleeding on the floor of the shop until an officer arrived, when I was jerked to my feet and carried off to a police station, but there being no evidence whereon to found and sustain a charge against me, I had my wounds dressed and bandaged and was then discharged.

Hastening to the rendezvous appointed before the action, I received at the hands of my companions in iniquity a hearty welcome, thanks, congratulations, praise and two big pies. This is a sad confession, but the pies were so good and I was *so* hungry.

I RECEIVE MY REWARD.

CHAPTER VI.

ANOTHER TURN OF, AND AT, THE WHEEL.

For another month or more I continued to lead the life, or existence, of a vagabond tramp in London, but at last I succeeded in shipping, as ordinary seaman, on board of a Hamburg brig, bound for Pernambuco, Brazil.

My peculiar and most undesirable luck by no means deserted me in this venture; the rest of the crew were all Germans and the strong antipathy then existing between these people and those of my nation, made my term of service in that craft resemble anything but a love feast, and kicks, blows, and polygot profanity was the order and exercise of the day until we arrived in port.

I had been doing my duty as cabin-boy, the only friend I had made on board was the mulatto cook, and we two, a hopeless and powerless minority, made up our minds to escape the continual unpleasantness by discharging ourselves, or taking "French leave" from the vessel.

Watching opportunity, we managed to bring round to the bow of the ship, and there secure one evening a small boat, and that night, during the cook's bow-watch, we dropped over the side, cast off our boat and pulled

PAYING TOLL.

for the shore, reaching the landing only to fall into the hands of a party of Brazilian soldiers; not incorruptible patriots, however, were these dusky warriors, and though the story of our woes, told in what of their language we could command, failed to melt their hearts and secure our liberty, yet a handful of copper coins, placed in their "itching palms," resulted in permission to go on our way rejoicing.

Just where we were to go, or how we were to get there, we had neither considered or discussed, but into the interior of the country, for safety from recapture, we knew we must strike; so, first finding the railway station, we started by following the track, and then plodded on for many weary miles, passing over many water courses. The yellow cook could speak English and a little Portuguese, but our fear of arrest made us very cautious and, deciding that the track of public travel was dangerous to our liberty we again sought the sea shore and followed this irregular path until we arrived at a little settlement, about twenty miles from our starting point.

Our reception here was by no means flattering, and we were not over-whelmed with welcomes. The inhabitants of the place were all fishermen, and their costume, or rather the want of it, was admirably adapted to a "header" into deep water at a moment's notice. There was one individual in the lot of natives, who had a leather shoe string from which dangled two sea-shells, tied about his neck, but public estimation evidently set him down as a dandified overdressed exquisite, for he had no imitators among his fellow citizens.

These people were equipped with some old muskets and all car-

AN OVERDRESSED NATIVE.

ried wicked looking spears or lances of home manufacture. They seemed to at once comprehend our situation, and without wasting time in explanations, they at once surrounded and marched us to a corral, guarded by six men and their families. Here we were put under surveillance as prisoners. Large fire were then built and kept up all night, and as I had rather sensational ideas about all savages and their habits, I concluded that I had indeed escaped "from the frying pan" to meet a more dismal fate.

But morning came and found us both unbarbecued, and shortly after daylight we were placed in the midst of a band of our captors and made to tramp disconsolately back to the place from which we had started. Here the cook claimed and found protection from the French Consul. I was kept away from him, and being unable to speak a word they could understand, or comprehend anything that was said to me, I was in a bad way, but I managed to let them know of my nationality by pointing to a Danish flag pictured on a chart, and I was then taken before the representative of that power, to whom I related my story.

Little good did it do me to meet this gentleman from Denmark; he railed at me in no measured language.

"You have no right to claim protection," said he; "you leave your country and your flag without permission, to enter and serve on a foreign vessel, and from this also you desert. I can and will do nothing for you except to send you back to the ship you run away from."

COLD COMFORT—HOT TALK.

"I will not go!" said I.

"Yes, you will go!" he answered.

"I'll die before I'll go back to that ship," I replied, all the stubbornness in my nature now fully aroused.

"Suit yourself about that," said the official, "but dead or alive, I'll send you back to that vessel."

And then I was put between guards and walked off to the citadel or military prison, and for the first time in my life found myself behind the bars. But the quarters were far more to my liking than being confined in the hold of the ship from which I had escaped, and such would have been my fate had I consented to return. In the citadel I had nothing to do, and was furnished two excellent meals each day, so I was comparatively contented.

But I was not destined to long enjoy my pic-nic, only too soon I was again taken before the Consul, heard his commands repeated, returned thereto my former reply and was again dismissed with the information that I would "have to go back."

And back to the ship I did go ; four strong sailors seized and tied me, tumbled me into a boat and took me to the side of the vessel. I was unbound and told to mount the ladder and go on board. I refused to move hand or foot in such direction, and finding that coaxings and curses were equally unavailing, a rope was put about my body and I was hoisted like a kicking mule and thrown on the deck I had vowed never again to touch. Little mercy and prompt punishment was the rule upon which worked

I RETURN TO MY SHIP.

the power to which I had been surrendered, and it seemed that I, who had declared that I would die before I would go back, was to be given ample opportunity to do that same after my enforced arrival.

With violent blows and curses I was driven into the sail room and there left in solitude, to end my life, it appeared, by starvation and thirst. For seven days I was kept in this solitary confinement without a morsel of food or a drop of water. Had it not been that I discovered a barrel of vinegar stored away in the room, I should certainly never have survived ; by soaking up with a piece of canvas the fluid that escaped from a leak in the cask, and then sucking the moist rag, I obtained sufficient nourishment to keep me alive, and such was all I had to sustain me during an entire week.

LIGHT DIET. DARK QUARTERS.

Though I became fearfully emaciated, and had hardly strength to speak or move, yet my spirit of resistance continued powerful as when in health and at liberty, and I still returned defiant refusals whenever the captain proposed that I return to duty and acknowledge his authority. At last, enraged though he was at my obstinacy, he became alarmed at my rapidly sinking condition, and, not from any humane considerations, but solely through fear of consequences to himself, he summoned a doctor who rated him soundly for his brutality and ordered my immediate removal from the sail room to more comfortable quarters and proper attention.

So far gone was I with starvation, that at first it was necessary to use great caution in feeding me, and three spoonsful of chicken·broth, given every fifteen minutes, was the allowance upon which I was rationed for a time. But a naturally robust constitution and light heart, soon braced me up to stand more substantial diet; appetite and strength returned, and in ten days I was almost as well and strong as ever, and with renewed health came fresh controversy, the captain continually urging or bullying me to go to work consentingly, and I as constantly refusing.

At last, knowing a sI did, that I was amenable to law for refusing to do duty, and seeing no way to obtain release or escape from the ship, I made a bargain with the captain, that if he would promise that all past quarrels should be considered as settled, and no prosecution ever brought against me for desertion, I would agree to do my part as one of the crew; and the contract was agreed upon; with the mental reservation on my side, that I would quit the ship again the moment I had a chance without danger of certain recapture.

Holding steadily to my determination, I once more took my place and worked hard in helping to load an invoice of sugar, with which we sailed to Parnahiba to take in the balance of our cargo. But the irrepressible conflict between the captain and myself soon again broke out with fresh violence. He first asked and then ordered me to cook ; as I had shipped as an ordinary seaman, and had no inclination to accommodate him in any way, I positively refused to comply with his request or to obey his command.

"I'll make you do it!" said he, with oaths and threats.

"You can't!" said I, with dogged obstinacy.

And as the skipper had always found that forcing me to do anything cost much more than the service was worth, he swallowed the affront and his dignity, took the back track and a boat, went on shore, brought off a cook and left me enjoy my victory and proper place as a sailor.

With others of the crew I had to go each day in a boat about a mile up the shore from where the ship lay to obtain a supply of fresh water. These trips seemed to me to offer a favorable opportunity for escape and I prepared to attempt it. Each trip we made I would take something with me, and in a few days I had secreted in the brush near the place where we obtained water, an extra shirt, an oil skin coat and as many ship's biscuits as I could lay hands on and carry off without exciting suspicion.

Though I was constantly looking out for a chance to slip off, there was none offered until the day that our ship was to weigh anchor and sail. I knew that the captain was suspicious of my intentions, and had ordered all the crew to keep close watch over me, but, just before sailing, two Englishmen, deserters from their own vessels, had been added to our force, and as my leaving would not make the ship short-handed and relieve him of a constant antagonist, I thought the captain was less anxious to keep me, and would thank any action or accident that would take me off.

At all events, on the day of departure, just as we were ready to make sail, I told the captain that I had left my oil skin coat near the watering place and asked permission to be set ashore and go after it.

"Go quickly and hurry back," was his answer.

This was the last order he ever gave me. I went quickly and I hurried, but in the opposite direction from the ship and its detested master was my line of march, and it would have taken a swift man to catch and a strong one to force me to return from the slavery from which I was escaping.

My hidden treasures I found all safe, and gathering them together, with a light heart and free heels, I struck out into unknown regions.

For days I steadily tramped on my solitary journey ; sometimes I would meet a native and try to communicate with him, but as I could only point to the southwest and say "Pernambuco," and the native could only point in the same direction and re-echo the word, the interchange was neither entertaining or instructive, though the manner of their pantomime and utterance of the word seemed to me to indicate that my destination was a long way off.

Many, weary and dreary were the miles I plodded over, with only the sun and stars to guide me on my way, through heavy mud and stifling dust, beat upon by heavy rain or roasted by a burning sun, and half crazed through hunger and thirst. One day I reached, I do not know when or how, the borders of a vast forest, and blindly I plunged into its depths, following the almost indistinguishable bridle path or narrow horse road that alone formed anything of a highway ; my only companions were the reptiles of all descriptions that continually appeared before me ;

parrots, monkeys and birds of every plumage were there in countless multitudes. Once my way was obstructed by an immense snake ; it was, I

A SIDE SHOW FREE.

think, fully thirty feet long, and to my eyes, then, it seemed ten times that extent. I am not positive of its size, as I did not stop to interview or measure it. I was in a hurry to get on. I got.

I had little or no idea how or when I would "fetch up." I knew that if I kept on the little trails leading in a southwesterly direction, and did not die on the way, I would eventually reach Pernambuco; so I marched on, not very steadily or strongly now, forcing my way through jungles of rank vegetation, fording slimy, sluggish bayous, and broad, swift, breast-high rivers ; my feet swollen to twice their natural size, and cut and blistered in a hundred places, had made it impossible to wear and useless for me to carry my shoes, and I had thrown them away long since ; my stock of food was reduced to three biscuits, not sufficient to sustain life for half the time I had yet to travel to reach port, so far as I could calculate. That was the fix I had put myself into, but still I was satisfied with my action in leaving that ship, and felt, even under such very adverse circumstances, that I was glad I had done it, and if ever I was similarly situated, "I'd do it again!"

On, and on, and on I hobbled, and just when my last crumbs of food were exhausted and hope almost gone, I staggered into a little native settlement. Such was my miserable condition that it excited the pity of an old Indian, who, with his squaw, proved good to be good Christians in deed if not in creed ; they found me a wanderer in a strange land, sick, poor, and sore wounded. They took me in, anointed my torn and bruised feet with oil, fed me with farina and crabs, gave me care, rest and shelter, and so patched up and strengthened me that in three days I persisted in resuming my journey.

The right road and direct course to Pernambuco having been pointed out to me by my good Indians, I followed the example of the soul of old John Brown, and kept ''marching along,'' refreshed in body and spirits by my late rest. After a few days' travel I came, in a lucky hour, upon a caravan of merchants, with slaves, parrots, monkeys, saffron and other products of the land, making for the same harbor as myself.

By sign language or pantomine, I gave these people to understand that I was a shipwrecked sailor who had been cast ashore many miles up the coast, and they appeared to be perfectly satisfied with my explanation. I noticed that when they prayed, as they did frequently, they repeatedly made the sign of the cross, so I was careful to often appear as though engaged in my devotions and to imitate their symbolic movements, and this soon attracted, as meant it should, their attention and they jumped at the conclusion that I was a faithful son of Mother Church, to whom it was their duty to render all aid and comfort; fortunate it was that they could not catechize me.

I was equally ready to be considered as Catholic, heretic, Turk or Pagan, and to adopt all outward signs of any religion if by so doing I could only get to my destination more quickly and easily. These kind people gave me food, put me on a horse, and cared for my still tender feet, until we arrived at the outskirts of Pernambuco, and there we parted, they bestowing upon me their blessings and a Brazilian dollar, wherewith I started the world afresh.

CHAPTER VII.

IN BRAZIL. ALL SORTS OF LUCK.

The events recorded in the last chapter occurred in the Summer of 1858, and it was then I first entered the town of Pernambuco as my own master.

A few hours after my arrival, as I was sauntering in rather a listless way about the place, who should I run afoul of but that same Danish Consul who had refused to aid me, and through whose orders I had been returned to the hateful ship. He seemed even more astonished than myself at the meeting.

'' What, you here ! '' he exclaimed, in tones not expressive of delight.

''Yes, I'm all here,'' I replied, coolly.

'' I'll have you arrested again,'' said he, with anger.

''I don't care if you do,'' answered I, '' you can't put me on that ship anyhow, she's far enough away from here now.''

He turned and walked off, muttering to himself, and I never was troubled by him again.

There was no vessel in that port on which I could ship, and so I looked about for other work. The English inhabitants of the town were building a gas works, and there I easily obtained employment as a laborer at three *millreis* ($1.50) per day. I toiled faithfully for about two months, drawing of my wages only sufficient for the most frugal living, and leaving the balance for accumulation in the hands of the foreman ; but when, after that length of time, I asked him for my savings, he flatly denied that he held a penny of my money or owed me anything, and settled the matter by discharging me on the spot as an impudent, dishonest swindler.

I could get no redress by law. My luck, as usual.

My blunders brought me into other troubles while at the Port, though the results were not so serious as the loss of my money.

I had reason to be very grateful to persons of the Catholic faith, who had proven themselves truly Catholic in their humanity and generosity to me ; and under no circumstances would I ever knowingly insult or outrage the religious sentiments of any person, be their creed what it might; so it was through ignorance, want of quick perception and general greenness that I got into two scrapes in Pernambuco.

A day or two after reaching the place, I was standing idly on the road side, when there passed along one of those church processions so common

IGNORANT IRREVERENCE.

in that land; priests and boys, banners and drums, etc., etc. In this case there was one priest who carried a crown of thorns covered with flowers, it being the symbol of that particular festival, and the people all reverently uncovered their heads, kissed the crown when presented to them, and gave in their contributions of small coin.

When this sacred emblem was presented to me, I did not exactly understand what exact course the etiquette of the occasion demanded, but anxious to follow, so far as possible, the motions I noticed, I removed my hat, inclined my head, and took a good *smell* of the flowers, and, as I raised my head and carelessly tossed over a small coin, which I could illy spare, I suppose I must, by "sniff" of nose, general manner, or some expression of face, have expressed my unspoken opinion that the *smell* was not worth the price, for, without in the least intending it, I had, by ignorant irreverence, excited the anger of processionists and spectators alike.

Whew! what a storm I had raised, my little coin was flung violently back into my face, my countenance was drenched with expectorations of the bystanders, and with a hearty good will did the holy father curse me and all my ancestors back to Adam, for heretics and devils, while the entire flock re-echoed, endorsed and amplified the anathematism.

That was my first lesson in church discipline, but not my last, for soon after I met another procession, in which a priest was bourne in a chair; banners were flying, surpliced boys chanting, rockets firing, censors of burning incense swinging, horns sounding, and drums beating; all hands in their finest holiday array. Evidently it was some very grand occasion, and I, anxious to take in all the free show possible, was gaping, open eyes and mouth, at everything so intently, that I did not notice that every man about me stood with uncovered and bowed head, while I, hat on and erect, was the conspicuous exception. But my prominence was not of honorable distinction, or long continued. I did not take my hat off, it was knocked off; I did not prostrate myself, I was knocked down, and then I was kicked up; everybody that could reach any portion of my anatomy with their feet, applied their boots thereto with most religious zeal which, with

CHURCH DISCIPLINE.

the curses again showered upon my head, quickly convinced me that I had once more offended against the laws of society and church.

It was a grand puzzle for my heavy brain; the first time I had been reviled and thumped for following, so far as I could, the example set me; and here I was knocked about, kicked and cursed because I did nothing at all. From that time I ceased to have the least interest in such processions and if I observed or fancied I saw any signs of one within a mile of me, I made a quick march in the opposite direction.

Robbed of my money, and employment being hard to obtain, I was forced to pass some days in idleness, and one morning, as I was sauntering about, I noticed that I had become a subject of close inspection to a man who followed me for some time. My curiosity was excited, and I soon gave him an opportunity to address me.

" Young mon," said he, and his tongue did not belie the unmistakable story of his features ; "Young mon, maybe it moigt be thot its wourk yer lookin' fur."

" Yes," I replied, so well as I was able, " I want work."

"Will, I'm runnin' ov a plantashun, 'bout foour moile back in the onterior, an' I'm wantin' a stout chunk ov a lad to tind till mathers ginnerally, an' kape the nagurs till ther wourk. Ye seems till be a likely chap, an' I wouldn't moind thryin' ye, ef ye feels till catch hould."

" Any port in a storm," thought I, so I soon managed to come to a understanding with the **FROM THE "ONTERIOR."** Hibernian gentleman, spite of the struggles between the two lingos, and in a few hours' time I found myself on his place in the " onterior," duly installed as " chief cook and bottle-washer, captain of the niggers," to quote the words of the old song.

There were seven slaves placed under my charge, and besides overseeing these, I had various other duties to perform. The most important of my work was in preparing a kind of sugar cake which my master sold in very considerable quantities. For a time all went well, I worked hard and gave full satisfaction to my employer until bad luck again grappled me and I caught, or was caught by, the yellow fever.

For two weeks I lay sick, nigh unto death, in stupor and delirium. All the care and medical attendance I received was from the proprietor, who, three times a day would force a pill down my throat ; it was a pellet of Yankee manufacture; I regret that I cannot recall the name and give it a gratis advertisement; but through its agency or the intervention of that Providence which guards babies, fools and drunken men, I contrived to get the better of Yellow Jack, and regained strength to potter about and look after the slaves, but unable to do any other work.

There was one of the gang, a big, lazy fellow by the name of Emanuel, whom I used to stimulate to quick finishing of his regular and prescribed stint of day's work by permitting him to go afterwards at easy jobs. One day he had completed his task in the field about half an hour before night and I had allowed him to leave the gang. Before all stopped, along came the boss.

" Whar's thon lazy nagur, 'Manu'l ? " he inquired.

"His day's work is done, and I let him quit," I answered.
"An' phat are the loiks of ye, thaot's till jidge whin his wourk's done

"CAPTAIN OF THE NIGGERS."

an' whin till quit. Sure an' I'll hev no shurkin wid ye ner th' nagurs,
th' wourk ov none ov yez so iver done whoile ther's th' loigt o'day till do't
in. Ye'll be plain' none ov yer bourd-ship sailoor thricks ontil me, ye
Dutch loafer ye ! "

The Irishman had been drinking and felt "ugly ; " he had come out
to find fault and worked himself into a passion in a moment. This injustice and abuse aroused my anger, and I returned a rather warm answer to
his tirade ; one hot word led to another, and at last he made an attempt to
strike me. I had learned to return such arguments in the same style, and
a healthy scrimmage was organized in a moment, in which, though much
reduced in strength, I would certainly have come off first best, had not the
servile blacks answered the call of their master and joined forces with him
against me, who had ever been their best friend, and with such reinforce-
ments he managed to give me a sound thrashing.

It was the old story—injustice, a fight, a beating and loss of employment ; but he paid me my wages, what little there was due me, and the
next morning sun beamed down upon me wandering once more about the
highways and byways of Pernambuco, a point to which I seemed naturally
to gravitate.

Willing and anxious to work, I jumped eagerly at the first offer and
engaged as "greaser and wiper " of machinery on an old trading vessel, the
PASSANUNGA, in which vermin infested tub I visited all the way ports
along that coast as far as the Amazon river, meeting with no adventures
worthy of record, "greasing and wiping " for my bread, without butter,

until January, 1859, when my services being no longer required, I was once more adrift and idle in Pernambuco.

Just as my little store of money was running out, and I had begun to despair of finding work, there arrived in port the Delaware river steamer MARY COMET, temporarily in the service of the United States, and attached to the Paraguyan Expedition. The vessel was, fortunately for me, short-handed, and on application I was shipped among her crew as an ordinary seaman ; my first enlistment under the Stars and Stripes.

We sailed to Rio Janeiro to coal, and then to St. Catharines, from thence to Monte Video, and at that place I was detailed as interpreter for the officers when they went on shore, I having contrived to pick up enough of the language during my residence in the country, to make myself understood.

My propensity for bringing trouble upon myself soon made it warm for me in the MARY COMET. I had been regularly placed among the crew of the shore boat, and considered that I

UNDER THE STARS AND STRIPES. was exempt from certain work on the ship, so one. day when the bo'swain's mate ordered me to sweep the deck, I bluntly answered, "I won't do it."

This terrible offence and incipient mutiny was at once reported to the commander, Lieutenant Walsh, and I was duly hauled up before that high authority.

"Did you refuse to sweep the deck when so ordered ? " he asked.

"Yes, I did ; it was no work of mine," I replied.

That is the full report of the proceedings of my trial ; the sentencing of the prisoner occupied about sixty seconds more.

"My man, you have violently outraged the rules and regulations, discipline and good order of the United States Navy by refusing to obey the orders of your superior officer. Double irons, bread and water and confinement in the hold will probably make you willing to do your duty. Mast'r Arms, take him down."

Double ironed I was, confined in the stifling hold also, and on bread and water, not an over-allowance either, was I rationed. The confinement and starvation troubled me little, a lashing I would have considered as quite a matter of course but the disgrace of being handcuffed like a felon, nearly broke my heart, and the misery welled up from my breast and found outlet through the ports of my eyes; I blubbered like a baby and begged hard for forgiveness and release. But the sentence was carried out in full and all the consolation offered me was the jeering of my shipmates and sarcastic inquiries as to how I liked Uncle Sam's jewelry.

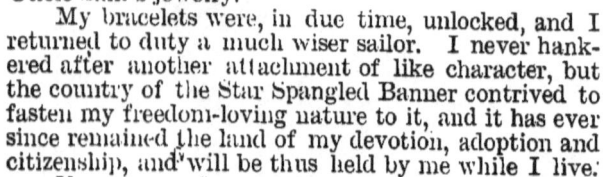

My bracelets were, in due time, unlocked, and I returned to duty a much wiser sailor. I never hankered after another attachment of like character, but the country of the Star Spangled Banner contrived to fasten my freedom-loving nature to it, and it has ever since remained the land of my devotion, adoption and citizenship, and will be thus held by me while I live.

Here many of us spent our shore leave and money in hiring riding horses and trying to stick on them, much to the amusement of the lookers on, our own danger of serious damage, and the misery of the animals.

U. S. JEWELRY

Horses are not high at Monte Video. The hire was $1 per half day. We were told that if we killed the horses it would be all square provided we brought back the saddles. The riders were hardly long enough on the "upper deck" at any one time to do much damage to the brutes.

After remaining about two weeks at Monte Video with others, I was transferred to a small tender named the WILLIAM II. CHAPIN, and in it we sailed for Philadelphia, Pennsylvania, arriving there about the first of May, 1859, and from deck I stepped for the first time upon the soil of the Great Republic of the earth. Almost immediately our vessel was ordered to Washington, where the crew was paid off and discharged, I receiving as balance due me the sum of twenty-eight dollars.

CHAPTER VIII.
CRUISING ON SHORE.

As became me, being now a free man in a free country, I put on my considering cap and reckoned up the best way in which I should proceed to make my fortune.

The path of the sea, which I had been following, did not seem to lead to wealth of great magnitude or very exalted station and I concluded that I would try the overland route to riches and honor. I purchased a suit of "shore togs" and made my way by rail from Washington to Philadelphia, and started out through that city in search of employment.

The two years of service or apprenticeship at the foundry in my native land had of course taught me something of the trade and I possessed sufficient knowledge to enable me to perform some of the rougher work. I obtained a place at North's foundry, Second and Mifflin streets, and was set at making covers for the old-fashioned cast-iron Dutch ovens; but the other journeymen soon discovered that I had never served my full time of apprenticeship and they combined to throw me out. By tricks, well known to the trade, my work was constantly spoiled, and at length they notified the foreman, and he informed me, that I could only remain there by entering as an apprentice or doing common laboring work. I accepted the latter alternative, but breaking up old iron,

43

I DON'T LIKE IT.

wheeling heavy pigs of metal, and loading rusty "scrap," was by no means to my liking, and after a week's trial, I resigned.

Through application made at an intelligence office, I next obtained a place as Jack-of-all-work, at a summer boarding house, about fifteen miles in the interior of New Jersey; wages, six dollars per month, and I remained there just long enough to earn that amount; then the idea of going West "to grow up with the country," that had found its way into my head, some time before, took such strong hold upon me that I was unable to stay in content where I was.

Back to Philadelphia I went, and at Dock street depot I purchased an emigrant's ticket for Cleveland, Ohio, and reached that place safe and sound with my plans for the future as indefinite as ever. My ideas as to the geography of this country were decidedly mixed and foggy, and so, when I noticed in the dock at Cleveland, a steamer on which I spelled out the word "BUFFALO," I reasoned that she must naturally and necessarily come from and go to the place where those animals made their home; that their haunts were in the wild far West I knew, and great was my delight when I found that not only could I go on her, wherever she was bound, and steam was up; but I was also told that I could go free of payment provided I shovelled coal during the trip. I seized the opportunity and the shovel with avidity.

Judge of my disgust when I found after starting, that the BUFFALO belonged in and was bound for the city of that name, in the State of New York, and when I arrived there I was about as far from the bison and the prairies as when in New Jersey.

But still intent upon reaching the land of the setting sun, I continued my efforts in that direction, and succeeded in shipping as seaman on the schooner C. BAKER, bound for Port Huron, on Lake Erie. In this craft I had a good time and pleasant associates; the food was first-class and plenty of it; there was a woman cook on board, and the men were treated like men. Had it not been for the demon of unrest which urged me on, I should have remained on the BAKER, but I had said to myself, "Go West, young man, go West!" I so went.

Leaving the schooner at Port Huron with good spirits

PRETTY WELL FIXED.

and two dollars in pocket, I struck out "on the tramp," and in that manner of progression I reached Sandusky, Ohio, and after trying and failing to find work or better means of transportation, with heavy heart and feet, with pockets completely lightened of cash, I footed it onward towards Toledo.

By this time I had become in look entirely, and in feeling somewhat, a genuine "tramp," a *professional*, and at that age the vagabond in my disposition seemed to reach its full development. I certainly did not dislike my occupation, or rather my life without one. When I was hungry I would keep a sharp look out for a farm that gave evidences of very careful attention, as though full handed, at its house I would apply for *work*, and as they had no work for me to do, they could not and never did refuse me food; in this manner I obtained what rations I required without being directly a beggar.

My education in my last *profession* soon advanced sufficiently to suggest improved means of locomotion, and I proceeded to try "jumping" the freight trains. By crawling into a car and secreting myself among a load of lumber, I managed to be carried to Chicago, where, with intent to pursue the same tactics, I hid in a train just starting and kept out of sight until the car, in which I was, had been detached and left at the station to which it was consigned; then I crept out and found that I had been taken on the back track East as far Indianapolis, Indiana.

EN TRAMP FOR TOLEDO.

Disheartened but not dismayed, I again turned my face to the West and started to recover the retraced miles. For a time I "jumped the trains;" when I was detected by the conductors or brakesmen, I would be put off and have to wait until the next train passed. I generally rode some considerable distance before discovery, and so saved many hours of foot travel while enjoying a boost on the car bumper. But transportation was not every consideration; there were very few houses directly on the line of the rails and the cars would not "stop for refreshments" for my benefit. It was a case of legs or stomach—one of these had to suffer, and stomach won the day. I abandoned car riding for the time being, except as an occasional luxury, and took up the tramp through country roads.

A BOOST ON THE BUMPER.

I did not want work, anyhow, not until I got "away out West," whither I was bound; but I did stand most terribly in need of cash and clothing. I had not quite lost all sense of shame or pride and I could not reconcile myself to the thought of coming down to what I considered straight, square begging, though the means I adopted and the results attained would hardly be called by any other name by an unprejudiced reasoner.

I still had in my possession, one poor, solitary little coin, a silver three cent piece, and on this remarkably light specie basis I operated, supplementing its power with various "ways that are dark and tricks that vain," practised by the tramping fraternity, and contrived to make that one piece of money find me in food for weeks without begging.

The *modus operandi* was as follows: I limp up to a house, and with doleful aspect and all the politeness I could muster, I would salute its mistress.

"Lady," I would say, and if the woman was particularly old, ugly and slatternly, I was careful to address her as "*young* lady."

"I am a poor man hunting for my friends who live somewhere about this neighborhood. I am very tired and very hungry, but I do not want to beg. I have just these three cents left in the world, will you please give me a few bites of food for it!"

That "fetched 'em, every time," the grub would be forthcoming, good and plenty. And who could be so heartless as to take the last three cents from a poor, foot-sore sailor lad?

Once, however, my financial resources were in very serious danger; they were for a short period actually sequestered. That was a terrible time to me, terrible!

I had stopped with the usual sorrowful tale and humble solicitation at the house of an old lady who served me with a moderate ration, and when I tendered to her my money, *she took it*. I was thunderstruck and demoralized; all my capital squandered for a "hand out," far below the general average as to both quantity and quality. The shock made me so sick that I almost returned the food I had eaten, on the spot.

But wild despair quickened my invention, and I determined to make a desperate effort to recover my treasure. Turning a really piteous face towards the dame, I said, with stimulated sobs and unfeigned sorrow:

"I am very thankful to you, lady, I must limp on now. Bless you, ma'am, bless you! May the time never come when you, or any one belonging to you, will ever have to turn from a door, out into the wide world, feeling that they have parted with their last cent, for food to keep from starving, and not knowing that they will ever have a crust given to them elsewhere."

And then, having worked up my own feelings into the belief that I was really a much injured mortal, and in immediate danger of death from the cause mentioned, I "bo-ho-ed" right out, in good earnest.

The appeal, the tears, were too much for the ancient madam who had begun, probably, to feel some shame in yielding to her cupidity; my three-cent piece was returned to me, and, proud tribute to my histrionic and oratorical powers, a dime was added. I was further filled up with a hugh wedge of pie and sent on my wicked way rejoicing.

The above was but one of the many incidents that tended to make my life on the road a series of singular, sometimes pleasing, and often exciting encounters. All sorts of people I came in contact with and each

individual had to be met and managed in a different way. "Blarney," the "taffy," of talk, was, on most occasions, the "best holt," and many were the times when a blousy servant girl, or vinegarish mistress, proposed to set the dog on me that a speech, complimentary to the charms of face or person, would keep the dog chained up and gain for me a square meal with milk in plenty.

I led this life for considerable time, and though my morals were fast becoming as seedy and dilapidated as my clothing and boots, yet my conscience, not

THE TRIUMPH OF GENIUS.

entirely dead to good, or my sense of manhood which still occasionally rebuked me, at intervals prompted the turning of my feet into a new and more honorable path, and at last such inward urgings, with the fact that I had seen enough of the West to be disenchanted for the time being, forced me to come to a right about and return to Philadelphia.

CHAPTER IX.
FRESH AND SALT.

Eastward bound once more, I made what haste I could to carry out my newly formed intention, and of course the country had to supply my wants as I travelled through it.

One morning as I was passing an orchard, the tempting sight of delicious apples upon the trees, and my hungry stomach, got the upper hand of my honesty, and I was soon among the fine fruit. I had eaten my fill and bundled a lot of choice specimens in my handkerchief and was about to take my departure when I was confronted by the angry proprietor.

"You confounded thief!" he cried, "I'll make you pay for those apples with your hide. I'll break your thieving back for you, you scoundrel!" and he flourished his stout cane to emphasize every word he roared.

It was all in vain that I pleaded my hunger and destitute condition, asked his pardon, offered to pay all the money I had for what was eaten, and to empty my bundle at the foot of the tree from which I had taken the fruit.

"No!" he would not be appeased; a thrashing I deserved and a thrashing he was going to give me. Now, in the navy I had, of course, taken my part in single-stick exercise; I quietly waited with the strong stick which formed part of my tramp equipment, until the old gentleman started to do execution with his cudgel, which he proposed to break over my head and back.

That I was in the wrong I was very conscious, and I resolved that my part in the combat should only be to defend my flesh and bones, and under no circumstances would I hurt the old man. So the first blow he struck was caught on my stick, and pound as he would, and he did his best, he could never break through my guard. I calmly parried all his cuts until he wore out his breath, his strength and his ill-humor all together; then he stopped and bade me take myself off and the apples with me, for an impudent rascal that I was.

FORBIDDEN FRUIT.

The fruit was very good, and a most opportune gift, as, the country just there being very thinly settled, I was forced to subsist upon it alone for two days.

In a hurry to arrive at Philadelphia, I "jumped" the cars at every chance, and finding that the "land-wrecked sailor" was the most "taking dodge," I "worked the racket" of a man-of-war's-man trying to get back to his ship, for all it was worth, and I found it a very valuable aid, even with those general unbelievers, the R. R. conductors. With my well concocted and oft-repeated story, I so worked upon the good nature of sundry trainmen that I was given many free rides and other favors, one man taking me through from Pittsburg to Altoona, and giving me a card to another who carried me to within three miles of Philadelphia, where I was obliged to drop off in order that he might run no risk of getting into trouble. I re-entered the Quaker City on foot, and hunting up some kind people I had before made friends with, I was by them furnished with food and shelter.

On application at the Navy Yard, in Philadelphia, I found that no sailors were being enlisted there, and I at once started for, on foot, Baltimore, Md., to try and ship from that city. From a "land-shark" who, in the hope of obtaining some of my advance pay, had helped to fix me up in somewhat presentable shape, I had gotten a pair of shoes; as it was not my fault that I could enter service at the first named place, I kept on, and walked off with, the shoes; but they proved the instruments of punishment for the wrong I committed, for being much too small, their pinching and the hard tramping so crippled my feet, that it was in terrible misery I marched on, and just below Wilmington, Delaware, I was forced by my sufferings to halt.

Stopping at the first house I came to, I asked leave to rest awhile and begged the people to give me a little food. In talking to the good lady I told her my true story, and as some of her ancestors had been Danes, she was so much pleased to meet a *bona fide* native of Denmark, that she treated me with most generous hospitality, and on my departure gave me a quarter of a dollar, the possession of which seemed to lessen very considerably the misery in my feet.

When near Perryville I concluded to take a rest by riding "a quarter's worth" in the cars, and at that place I waited for and boarded the train. The rear cars were occupied by a militia company, on an excursion to Baltimore; I crowded in among the merry holiday soldiers, and, as we steamed rapidly over the miles, I waited in fear and trembling for the conductor to appear ; but that official never came, and I was taken into the city of Baltimore free of charge. Good luck for once.

I immediately made tracks for the shipping depot, and by sacrificing my two months' advance pay, twenty-eight dollars, to a land-shark, I was able to obtain the necessary outfit with which to pass the required inspection, and in a few hours I found myself snugly stowed away, an Uncle Sam's Blue Jacket, on board the U. S. Receiving Ship, ALLEGHENY, where I was duly instructed in the routine of duty, which, in port, is more monotonous than exciting, though my blunders managed at times to vary the even tenor of my way.

It was my fortune for a time to be "spit box" bearer ; that by no enviable position which is the reward, or penalty, bestowed for expectoration upon the deck. The man of mark, or who makes such mark, has the box strapped upon his breast, unpleasantly near, and directly under his

"SOME HAVE HONORS THRUST UPON THEM."

nose, and he is forced to walk the deck for the accommodation of the crew, and carry this unsavory load until he detects and reports some new offender in the same way. But the reporting does not always follow such detection, for if the guilty party latest discovered be the best man of the two, a tremendous thrashing is sure to follow the transfer of the badge of dishonor and dirt. I was forced to carry that detestable box for three days before I caught a fellow sinner whom I could report and whip also.

There was still another naval honor I had thrust upon me while on the

ALLEGHENY, it was the position *Captain of the Head;* this promotion is won by being found washing clothing at times other than those prescribed by the ship regulations. The duties of the *Captain* consist in cleansing a very necessary, but not particularly sweet-scented section of the vessel's internal economy. The occupant of the post has, as some slight compensation, the special privilege of washing clothing every evening, and as there are always plenty of lazy sailors, the ALLEGHENY had her share of them ; and as they would pay a shilling for washing a shirt, twenty-five cents for cleaning a hammock, and for other articles at proportionate rates, I made several dollars during my occupancy, which continued exactly one week, when I gladly retired in favor of some other unfortunate, who, by sin of omission or commission, was considered to have earned a right to the high (flavored) dignity.

While on this Receiving Ship I endeavored to improve my knowledge of and speech in the English language, and purchasing a spelling book I

 set earnestly to work, copying also the written characters. I made considerable progress in my self-imposed and difficult task and my perseverance excited the admiration of my shipmates to such an extent that two old tars, Billy Sims and Jack Fetty, veterans of the Mexican War, propose to aid me, so far as speech went, by slitting my tongue with the sharp edge of a silver shilling, which they assured me was just the thing to improve the talking of parrots and "furriners," and

AN AID TO THE ACQUISITION OF ENG- that "it wouldn't hurt a bit and
LISH.

do me a power of good." They siezed me and were about to carry out their plan when my howls brought the officer of the deck, who put an end to the experiment.

For six months I remained upon the vessel, then I was drafted for yard and boat duty at the Naval Academy, Annapolis, Md., from there in two weeks, transferred to the Receiving Ship PENNSYLVANIA, laying at Norfolk, Va., where I remained until the end of the year, when, tired of the dull, uneventful life, I asked for my discharge, which was readily granted, their being at that time too many men in the navy.

I received my discharge in October, 1860, and my pay amounted to exactly $128, being just one hundred dollars more than the sum with which I quitted my first U. S. ship. The Western fever had again taken possession of me, and I made ready to once more move in that direction, not however, as as tramp this time, but in a mild way, as a "bloated capitalist," a merchant, though my ideas in that line did not rise above the dignity of peddling.

50

CHAPTER X.

SUNDRY SHORE AND SORE SITUATIONS.

Doffing the blue and donning the "biled" shirt, with store-clothes corresponding, I travelled, as a gentleman of moderate means, not wealthy  but independent; from Baltimore to Wheeling, West Virginia, there took steamer to Cincinnati, Ohio, from thence going to St. Louis, Mo., where I secured boarding at the Green Tree Hotel. I was at that moment in possession of good health and strength, a serviceable knowledge of the English language, a pretty solid opinion of myself and abilities, a fair stock of clothing, one hundred dollars in cash, a varied experience, and a revolver, which weapon I bought by advice of a friend and was always afraid to handle for fear I should unintentionally blow the roof off my own or somebody else's head.

Seeing no immediate opening for judicious investment of my capital and being unwilling to remain in idleness which would reduce my store, I looked about for employment.

I had half formed the intention of taking an overland train for California, but it was the depth of winter and all lines of travel were blocked with heavy snows. The St. Louis and Missouri Pacific Railroad was at that time in course of construction and men were wanted to work upon the line, wages being $1.15 per day. This seemed better

WITH MONEY IN MY
POCKET.

than living "all out and nothing in," so I concluded to take up the pick and shovel as a railroad laborer and try to dig my way into a fortune.

Soon I was enrolled in a gang and forwarded to the place of work, which was where the town of Sedalia now stands; at that time the ground was an immense corn field, the whole section, bleak, barren and cheerless as the North Pole, cold as a pawnbroker's heart; a dull, gloomy, howling wilderness, the only building for miles about being the big barn of an "Irishman's shanty" erected for the R. R. workmen.

We had good, coarse food, and plenty of it, and far more than plenty  of bad whiskey, which could be bought for twenty-eight cents a gallon, and was of that quality that contained three drunks, six fights, oceans of profanity and any desired number of black eyes in every quart of it.

All around the four sides of the house were *shelves*, substitutes for beds, roosting places, called by a liberal stretch of courtesy and truth "sleeping bunks," and these

ENJOYING THEMSELVES.

reached from floor to roof. Every night the scenes performed in that sin-sodden shanty would have made Donnybrook Fair seem a Quaker meeting

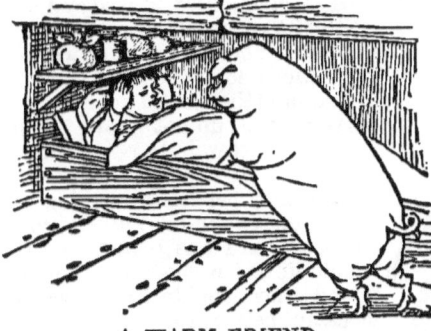

by contrast; the crazy-drunken crowd would dance, and fight and howl, and roar like all the fiends in Pandemonium. They called this "enjoying themselves."

Outside it was colder than zero, inside it was hotter than China, but in no wise so celestial. There was comfort for me neither inside or outside; because I would not join in the whiskey guzzling and insane devilment in which they delighted, these generous blackguards would give me my share of the liquor by

A WARM FRIEND.

throwing it into my face and eyes.

I wanted the work and the pay; as it only cost two dollars per week for board, so I was making and saving money, and though it was a horribly rough and unpleasant life, I was disposed to stick to it as long as I could. Cold and windy! I shiver yet when I think of it. It had been my luck to be assigned a bunk on the floor range, and the blasts that came sweeping in under the doors, and poorly joined weather boarding cut through me like a knife, the one thin blanket allowed me being hardly any protection whatever, and night after night I lay shivering and sick with the cold, awake through all the dark hours, until Providence came to me in the shape of a pig.

The person who boarded the laborers had a pig, and piggy with the wisdom of his kind, knew that it was much warmer inside than outside the shanty, so he got in the habit of seeking his repose within, and being a very sober and gentlemanly pig, he naturally sought out a human of somewhat the same characteristics. As I was the only temperance man in the party, and my ground floor bunk very handy, piggy chummed in with me, and after we found that by laying very close together there was a considerable amount of heat to be obtained for each from the other, we were constant bed-fellows and perfectly satisfied with each other, though sometimes he wanted more than his fair share of bunk room.

My success with the pick and shovel was not brilliant, that I lacked natural aptitude for effectively handling these valuable implements was was soon so apparent that the boss, who was not a bad fellow, changed my task and tried me as mule driver, and two of those

POOR PICKING.

long eared, nimble heeled embodiments of all cantankerousness were delivered over to my charge, or rather I was delivered over to their cussedness. Of all the mulish mules that ever backed, baulked, bucked, shied, kicked and bray-

ed, these two were the worst ever built upon four hoofs since mules were first manufactured. Whether I could not understand them or they could not understand me, I do not know; but just what I did *not* want those confounded mules to do was the very perfor- mance they persisted carrying out; this would excite my mulish propen- sities, and as I was bound that they should do as I wished, and they were bound they wouldn't, the war was incessant between us. But the other two mules always won.

THE THREE OF US.

How long my patience (or obsti- nacy) and perseverance would have enabled me to hold out in the fight be- tween us three, or how soon I would have been killed by the mules, or "bounced" by the boss, as incompetent, it is impossible to judge ; the blackest mule won the fight and settled the question most summarily, by bringing his hard hind hoof down upon my great toe with deliberate malice and sufficient force to crush the nail deep into the flesh and so cripple me that I was given an honorable discharge for wounds received and disability incurred in the line of duty, and, with earnings in pocket and foot in a sling, I returned to St. Louis.

While laid up, nursing my foot, I became acquainted with an old German, who induced me, so soon as I was able to again be about, to embark some of my capital in the manufacture of artificial honey, the substitute for the "bee- juice," being composed of genuine honey, wax and sugar. The senior partner prepared the stuff, and I peddled it to druggists and grocers at a price far below that of the real article. We were building up a good trade and making a fair amount of money, when our bright prospects were clouded and obliterated by the outraged honesty or some other motive of the Irish woman in whose house we lodged. This female follower of Saint Patrick spied in upon our manipulations, as we used her wash house for a laboratory, making, in a clothes boiler, the "genuine Bee-Honey," without troubling the busy bees in the least.

THE OTHER FELLOW WON.

In emphatic language and violent passion this Milesian madam venti- lated her opinion that we were a pair of "pizinin', murtherin', swindlin' Dutch vagabones," and wound up her tirade by shouting, hair and fist flying, "I'll put the perlice on ye! I will! I will!" and flung herself out as though intending to at once summon an officer.

I had a holy horror of all law proceedings and knew not how great was the extent of my offending or its penalty; and I had no particular desire for enlightenment on these points, so I quickly then and there dissolved the partnership and retired from the firm and its sweet business, with a loss of twenty dollars on my original investment.

CHAPTER XI.
THE LUCK IS MIXED.

Modest by nature and not desiring to be brought prominently before the public through police influences, my retiring disposition made me anxious to leave St. Louis at the earliest possible moment, and so I took passage on a steamboat bound for New Orleans, La., but we had only proceeded on our journey down the Mississippi as far as Cape Girardeau, when the boat stranded, the "cold snap" caught us, and for fourteen days we were ice bound at that point.

"I'LL PUT THE PERLICE ON YE!"

Always anxious to be earning something, when wood choppers were wanted to get together a supply for the boat, I applied to be put at the work. But I was no more an axe man than a pick expert and after inflicting several minor cuts upon my shins, which caused me to limp around in bandages, I put an end to my career as wood butcher, by sinking deep into my foot the sharp blade intended to split a great log of wood into size for the cabin stove.

Crippled and quiet I remained until the boat at last reached New Orleans, by which time I was again able to walk about. My cash on hand footed up about sixty dollars and fearing that, unless I at once engaged in some business for employment I could not find; my money would run off from me and I would run

NO HAND—BUT A FOOT—FOR EDGE TOOLS.

off to sea (which I did not wish to do), I plunged at once into a new and fowl business, the chicken trade.

I would carefully watch for and be first to board the flat boats that came down the river bringing market produce and truck for city consumption, from these I would purchase their entire stock of chickens, in large or small lots, then tramping around the streets with as many specimens of my stock as I could carry in my hands or hang about my person, I would sell them to restaurants, hotels and families, singly or by pairs, so many as they wanted, at a very fair profit.

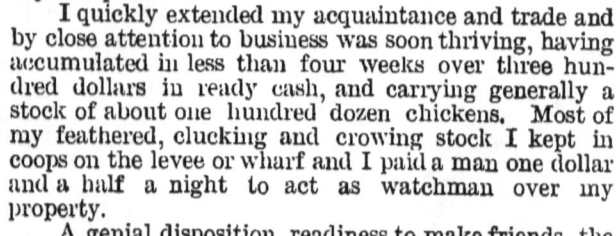

I quickly extended my acquaintance and trade and by close attention to business was soon thriving, having accumulated in less than four weeks over three hundred dollars in ready cash, and carrying generally a stock of about one hundred dozen chickens. Most of my feathered, clucking and crowing stock I kept in coops on the levee or wharf and I paid a man one dollar and a half a night to act as watchman over my property.

A genial disposition, readiness to make friends, the somewhat liberal use of money that was now rather plentiful in my pockets, any one, or all of these combined, served to make me really or apparently very popular with a certain class of individuals to be found everywhere, who are always glad to share any man's prosperity. I was soon "in with the boys" who made much of, and off me.

A FOWL TRADE.

This was in the " good old times," just " befo' the wa'," when gambling was openly carried on in hundreds of places in New Orleans and other cities of the South, where in magnificent apartments, with free suppers, liquors and segars for visitors, piles of glittering coin were hourly won or lost, and fortunes changed hands nightly. Into one of these establishments, on a second floor of a building near the French market I was introduced by several of my new found friends, and after the excitement and temptation had taken hold upon my imagination, it required little or no persuasion to induce me to venture my money.

The first night that I entered the lists against the tiger, "I won squarely or was allowed to win over forty dollars, and I left the gambling house perfectly intoxicated, not with liquor, but with my good fortune. Here was the right way to make money, to get rich! I had found the road to fortune at last, and I laid awake speculating how long it would take me, calculating my winnings at forty dollars a night, to become as rich as I wished to be. Well, I was a big fool, as there has been big fools over just the same alluring prospect since the earth was peopled, and will be big fools until the earth has ceased to exist.

The chicken business contained no element of excitement equal to my new found money making scheme, and, never realizing that I was but a poor chicken, to be most unmercifully plucked by the hawks that I had allowed to gather round me, I went a second time to the gambling place, not to fare quite so well as on my first visit. Then I went a third time, sure that I would make up my losses and win much more, and as I left the doors of the house that night, they closed on a room and table where I had parted with over two hundred dollars of my honestly earned savings which had gone to fill the pockets of my disinterested, newly found, very dear friends.

As I said before, the unhealthy and unnatural excitement of those last few days had caused me to neglect and despise my chicken business, and now that I begun to understand what a poor fool I had been, I thought it was time for me to look after the legitimate trade that brought me honest gains and good sleep. I hurried to the levee and reached the spot where I expected to find one hundred or more dozens of chickens, and I saw nothing. The space generally occupied by my stock was a bare, empty patch, not a coope, not a chicken, not even a feather to be seen and no watchman about. After considerable trouble, I found the man whom I had employed to guard my property, and discovered that he had ignorantly, or for a share of the proceeds, delivered the entire lot on a fraudulent order, signed by the name of a firm that had no existence, and there was not left to me a single chick or payment of a cent.

Utterly unmanned and driven frantic by this latest loss, crowded as it was upon my squandered capital left with the gamblers, I gave a howl of despair, cried, tore at my hair, and at last rushed to the edge of the levee and giving what I thought was my last yell of anguish on earth, I plunged into the Mississippi. All this occurred on my birth day, and the anniversary of my entrance into the world would have marked my exit therefrom, had I not been such a born blunderer that I could not even commit suicide properly.

Had I dived in my head would certainly stuck fast in the deep mud which underlaid the few inches of water about the part of the levee from which I made my plunge, and I would have found a dirty death through suffocation in the filth, but as I had *jumped,* it was my legs that sunk into the slimy, sticky, putrifying mass of refuse in which I sunk waist deep.

For the second time in my life the desire to end my existence was destroyed by the agency through which I attempted to accomplish the deed, and as I felt myself slowly sinking in the mass of corruption, I howled most lustily for aid, and was fished out or

ALL GONE.

dragged from the mire, to employ an hour or so in cleansing my person and garments and collecting for future service what of brains and common sense I was possessed.

My latest and most unpleasant experiences of life in New Orleans had rendered its atmosphere, and all connected with the city, most unpleasant. Had I won, instead of lost money by gambling, I dare say all would have been rose-colored, but I didn't win, and was therefore piously penitent as poor, so I gathered up my ideas and property, took in all money due me, and started for other pastures.

CHAPTER XII.

STILL ON THE DOWN GRADE.

When I scraped the mud of its dock from off my garments and shook the dust of the Cresent City from off my No. 12 brogans, I had no very definite idea of where I was going, but I took a steamer, and in three days during, which I gradually recovering a healthy state of mind, I found myself in Galveston, Texas, and there I fell in with an old friend and fellow countryman.

It was just at this time that the secession excitement had reached its red-hot temperature, "Lone Star" and "Palmetto" flags were fluttering from hundreds of halyards and poles, and the "Stars and Stripes" were conspicuous by their absence. On every side was heard the busy notes of preparation for grim war. The people of the South, men, women and children, were crazy "to fight for their rights ; " the steamer HARRIET LANE had been taken possession of by the State authorities. It was very evident that war and bloodshed was inevitable.

Men were then in all portions of the country, obliged to define their positions in very plain language, taking sides one way or the other, and asserting themselves boldly. There was no study over the question with me. Since I had left the flag of my native land, I had served under that of several other nations, but the "Flag of the Union" was the first that attracted the loyalty of my heart, before I ever heard of or knew the word secession, I had sworn allegiance to the starry banner, not only in words, but by true adoption for the balance of my life and to the old flag I was going to stick through thick and thin, on the relative merits of the questions in dispute between the two sections I did not try, or was I competent to form an opinion, I followed blindly the promptings of my first love.

Moved by such feelings and not bashful in giving expression to my sentiments, the sunny South was entirely too warm a climate for my general health, and I realized that I had better be making tracks for the North. My Danish friend's sympathies were decidedly Southern, and he was going to remain on that side of Mason and Dixon's line. Our personal

relations were as warm as ever, but we had some hot political discussions which were, as are most arguments of that character, mere gas over matters that neither of us knew the least about. We shook hands heartily when parting, and wished each all sorts of good luck to the other. I presented him with the revolver I had bought in St. Louis.

"Here, my brother Dane," I said, as I struck a heroic attitude, "take this to remember me by, but let me beg of you for the sake of our father-land to turn its deadly contents into

IN REMEMBRANCE.

your own brain, before you use it against the defenders of the glorious Flag of Liberty!"

I was most anxious to be on the move, and acting without thinking of the old saying, on the queer principle that "the longest way round is the nearest way home," I shipped on a coasting vessel to Pensacola, Appala-chicola, and other Florida points, and finally brought up once more in New Orleans with about forty dollars in my purse.

It was officially announced that March 14th was the last day on which a steamboat would be permitted to depart for the North. Two days pre-vious to that time I met a discharged soldier of the U. S. army, who was without means to get to his Northern home and friends, and going with him to the boat I secured and paid for his deck passage to Cairo, Ill. A well dressed, keen looking individual was standing near the clerk's office at the time and witnessed the whole transaction, hearing also the conversa-tion incident thereto; he saw my money and very probably overestimated the amount of it.

This gentleman, after a short time, approached and entered into con-versation with me, indulging in many very complimentary remarks re-garding my liberality, etc., to the poor soldier; "just what he had done himself hundreds and hundreds of times, he said," and as our acquaintance grew he became more and more "taken with me," and at last, I being "just the man he was looking for," he offered me a situation as overseer on his plantation at thirty dollars per month, house, horse, food, and no end of other inducements being included. His generosity was unbounded, and his political sentiments were, to a dot, the same as my own.

Thinking I had better secure such a good place until I could save more money, and trust to luck to get North when flush with cash, I promptly accepted his offer and we parted, but not, however, until I had promised to meet him at 2 o'clock of that afternoon, at the St. Charles Hotel, to take a ride in his carriage and give an opinion about a new pair of horses he had just purchased.

I was on time at the place of appointment to a minute; there was my new friend and employer, and there also was a fine team, with coach-man in livery.

With Chesterfieldian polite-ness, Mr. Spider invited Mr. Fly to enter the carriage; proudly I did so, and he, after saying a few words to the driver, seated himself beside me. He then explained that be-fore going out on the Shell road to the lake, for a good dinner, he wished to drive to the Alabama depot to arrange for sending to his hotel a trunk that was there, for which he had written to his mother.

I was only too happy to ride wherever he desired, and we tooled along to the depot, the gentleman

THE SPIDER AND THE FLY.

then left me but returned in a few moments with a check for $100 (or what purported to be such) in his hand and asked if I could change it. I expressed my regret that I had not so much money with me. He was much annoyed at the prospective trouble of coming back again, he wanted $13 to make up, with what small notes he had, the amount of his freight bill.

"Perhaps I could accommodate him with that trifling amount until he got his check cashed at the Lake Hotel, where he was well known."

"Certainly I could, and would."

And I did.

Then he stepped back into the depot, and I sat in the carriage and waited, and waited, and waited.

But he didn't come back.

After a good long while, coachman turned around, leaned down and over until he could see inside the carriage, and inquired if we "was agoin' to keep the hosses astandin' there all night."

"I guess you'll wait until your master comes back," said I, with dignity.

"Master be blowed!" replies Cabby, "that fellow ain't no master o' mine, I hain't got none. He's a *sharp*, that's wot that feller is, an' takin' a bird's eye view of it I should say he was a playin' you fur a *flat*."

And that worldly-wise driver further continued.

"But that ain't nothin' to me noways, sharps er flats, ripe 'uns or green 'uns, tain't none of my funeral. Wot I want to know is, ef you got the coin ter pay fer the hire o' this hack."

Then I became awake to the stern realities of my situation, and knew that I had been swindled. It was in vain I protested that I had not hired the carriage, had been invited to ride, etc., etc., Cabby remarked with firmness:

"Don't know ner keer nothin' 'bout that, this here hack an' them ther hosses hes been in use of you an' that other feller for over two hours. I ain't got him but I hev got you, an' I'm goin' to hev the hire of this hack an' them hosses er ther'l be trouble."

Sadly I paid him more than legal charges from my much diminished cash, and then, in a perfect fever of haste to quit a city where everybody and every action seemed to combine against me, I hurried to the levee, found the boat on which I had placed the soldier, secured a deck passage for myself, and was, an hour after, steaming away from the scene of my misfortunes and foolishness.

Travelling on a deck-passage ticket, I was not entitled to meals, and could buy no food on the boat, and in the hurry and excitement of getting away I had never thought to provide rations. When the boat stopped at Baton Rouge, I hurried into that town to purchase food, feeling confident that I had time to lay in a supply and get back before the boat took in coal, that being its regular station for so doing.

With a handkerchief well crowded with sundry eatables and a big loaf of bread under my arm, I returned to the landing place, but my boat was not there, and I could just manage to hail it and receive answer, short and pointed, to the effect that I could stay where I was. The steamer had started so soon as her freight for that place was landed and was taking in coal from a barge in tow at her side as she rushed away.

The loss of my fare and time was a very serious matter just then, but a still greater was that of my sailor's bag in which was all my clothing and  a diary, fully written up, in which was recorded the history of my adventures and ramblings, all these were now lost, carried away by that miserable steamboat that seemed to say in every puff, "Left! left! left!"

There was but one course of proceedings open to me which was to board the next steamer coming up. In an hour or two I was again on my way and dame Fortune did me one good turn on this trip by making the eyes of the clerk blind to my presence; that stern official never appearing to demand or collect my passage money. I didn't hunt him very anxiously, and so travelled to my destination D. H.

When I arrived in Cincinnati, Ohio, I was dirty to the last degree and certain "small deer," common among deck passengers, were making themselves entirely too familiar with my flesh and blood. I was disgusted at

LEFT.

my condition and sought to remedy it, so I purchased a cheap outfit of underclothing and then proceeded to the poor man's bath place, the river. The tower of the grand suspension bridge, which now spans the Mississippi at that point, was then about thirty feet high, and getting down under its protection from the wind, I proceeded to disrobe and afterwards to bathe in the intensely cold water, where the ice in blocks of all sizes was grinding sullenly together.

Certain persons had watched me as I made my way down to the water's edge, and when they saw me commence to undress, concluding that I intended suicide, they rushed to secure me, and it required considerable broken English from me to convince them that I really intended to only take 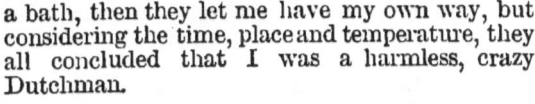 a bath, then they let me have my own way, but considering the time, place and temperature, they all concluded that I was a harmless, crazy Dutchman.

CHAPTER XIII.

A GOOD SAMARITAN.

My funds were now running very low; I had only about three dollars left—that this would soon be exhausted in Cincinnati I well knew. It was necessary that I should at once find work, but though I hunted industriously for it, I could not obtain employment in the city.

With my earthly all in a very light bundle, I made my way into the country and found that there was plenty of work, but none that I could do. It seemed as though I had to answer "No," to every question asked me.

"Could I work in the garden?" "No."

FOR SCOURING, NOT SUICIDE.

"Could I take care of horses?" "No."

"Chop wood?" 'No." "Milk cows?"

"No." and so on through an endless string of interrogatories with the same unvarying answer to all.

When asked "What can you do ?" I would reply "Nothing, only try to do as I am told."

Willingness did not seem to be considered as an equivalent for knowledge and skill however, and I tramped on through Hamilton county, until I came to Fairfield, Indiana, where I paid my last money, twenty-five cents for lodgings, and the same amount for breakfast, and then continued my wanderings, destitute of destination as of means.

Over roads that seemed to lead to nowhere in particular, and by turnings that faced me to every point of the compass, I pursued my weary way until I was brought to stand still on the banks of a small river. Though I had been a sailor and long lived close to deep water, yet I did not know how to swim. The barrier presented by this deep, rapid running water way, over which there was no bridge or signs of road leading to one, appeared to me to be a predestined halting place in my life, to which my erratic footsteps had been directed by an overruling Providence.

"Thus far and no further, in thy present course shalt thou proceed !" is what the rippling of the current seemed to sound within my ears.

What influences possessed me I know not, but there was some changeful process working powerfully within my mind. I asked myself, "What shall I do ?" knowing full well that I could invent no answer to the query. It really appeared as though I had reached the end of all things for me.

Then the words of my mother, spoken when I bade her "Good-bye," as I recklessly cast from me her protecting care, and blindly plunged into a world of which I was ignorant, came crowding back upon my memory.

"My son, trust to God, and make yourself worthy of his fatherly love; keep yourself pure, never lie, be honest, do your duty to your masters, be sober, pray to be kept in the right way, and against all trials and troubles, snares, wickedness, and dangers of this world, He will guard and hold you safe."

My mother was a woman always occupied busily with the cares of this life, who indulged in none of the sentimentality often found conspicuous in those who least practice what they preach ; but the true root of all good was in her, the knowledge of the way to peace and happiness she fully possessed, and the occasion on which she had spoken to me, her very words, were indelibly impressed upon my mind.

The recollection of this incident, with all its attendant circumstances, banished from my brain every feeling or sense, but that of the utter abandonment and desolation in which I now stood, and,

entirely oblivious of the peculiar position in which I was placing myself, I fell upon my knees, my eyes streaming with tears, hands clasped in agony, and with lips long unused to the language of devotion, in my native tongue, I poured out my petition to the Almighty for pardon, guidance, aid and protection.

What I said, how long I remained thus, I know not, so absorbed was I, so completely transported from all earthly considerations and surroundings, by the emotions of the hour, that even the noise made by the

BROKE DOWN.

arrival at the spot of a carriage, drawn by two horses, did not attract my attention, and when I at last returned to thoughts of mundane matters, I found myself the subject of curious contemplation on the part of an elderly gentleman seated in the vehicle which was standing close to me. His glance and air seemed not unkindly, and, as I sprang to my feet in great confusion he called to me.

"My boy," said he, "what is the matter?"

Now prayer had become, with me, such an unusual exercise, for years past, that I felt half ashamed to confess that I had been asking the help of God, and endeavored to evade answering.

My new acquaintance bade me jump into the carriage beside him, which I did; he then cautiously forded the river, and as he drove along, closely but pleasantly questioned me, skilfully leading me on into making confidences until, before we had travelled many miles, he was in full possession of the leading facts and incidents of my history, and I concluded by candidly acknowledging that, having felt myself powerless, and trusting no longer in my own strength or the mercy of man, I had gone to the Father above, and begged for help and comfort.

"And don't you think he sent it?" the old gentleman asked.

Soon he put the old question that I had so often answered.

"What can you do?"

And again came the ready, but most unsatisfactory answer, "Nothing."

IN REPLY.

For once this reply did not frighten or quiet my new friend who apparently argued that a man or boy, who was willing to admit that he could do nothing, might be learned to do something; and I doubt not but experience had taught him that those who professed to be able to do everything, frequently were incapable of anything; all of which complicated reasoning has come into my later understanding. I had the notion of it at that time but could not have expressed my ideas, and I am now giving the world the benefit of my matured wisdom.

Before we reached his destination, this man, whom I believe was sent in answer to my prayer, had bargained with me that I was to come and live with him, to be paid six dollars a month "and found," to do nothing until it was discovered that I was fit to do something.

The name of that good man I will here call, John Stuart, of Blankville, this also fictitious, Indiana, and that he never had cause to regret his generosity exerted in my behalf, it is my pride to feel conscious. I was, and am,—will ever be, very, very, grateful to him.

I went into his home, rough and ignorant, but ready and anxious to learn, and it is really wonderful how, in a short time, I did contrive to pick up and properly attend to many matters of greater or lesser importance, and all of which tended to get through more quickly with the routine work of the place, and save the backs, hands and feet of others. I learned, or commenced to acquire, in that comfortable home many things that were of great use to me afterwards, and I know that I did what was considered more than sufficient to repay the kindness that was ever exhibited towards me by each member of that family.

CHAPTER XIV.
I 'LIST FOR A "SODGER."

The war cloud which I had seen rising in the South had now increased in size and blackness, until it overshadowed with its gloom, every portion of our nation.

The first gun fired at Sumpter echoed and re-echoed throughout the world, and in our own land, from California to the borders of Canada, the men of the North waked from their apathy, and girded themselves for the dread work before them. My native land retained that portion of my affection which every man must ever feel for the country of his birth, but the United States was the nation I had chosen, of all others, to be *my* country, under the Old Flag I had served, and I was going to permit no one, American or foreign born, to exceed me in devotion and service to it, so far as it lay in my power to perform my duty.

There was work now that no one need ask me "Can you do it?" "Can you fight for the Stars and Stripes?" Every impulse of my nature and throb of my heart told me, "You *can* do it!" and I determined to go.

I had not been one month with my kind employer, I was happy, fully content in a good home, and knew that he and his family were entirely satisfied with me, but, unimaginative and stolid as my mind had ever appeared to be, I felt this to be a call direct to me.

The resolve "to go," meant everything in those days of national trouble. Mr. Stuart was in full sympathy with my patriotic fervor, and did nothing to deter me in my proposed action, and, on the 22d day of April, 1861, I signed my name and was enrolled in the company being raised by Captain John X, being the first recruit enlisted in the town of Blankville, Indiana.

My master endorsed and applauded me, but there was trouble in his household, nevertheless, over my 'listing. I had become much less bear like in my movements and manners, had also acquired a certain skilfulness about the farm work that was found of great service and Mrs. S. did not fancy the idea of losing the broad back and strong, willing hands, she found in her man of all work. Then there was a certain comely damsel in that house, whose bright eyes, glossy ringlets and pretty airs and graces, had excited my susceptible nature to an extent of which I was unconscious up to the time when in begging me not to "go," the water reservoirs of her pretty eyes freshened up the love germ in my heart until it grew and blossomed, with magic celerity into a most flourishing plant.

But I had pledged my word to others and to myself, and honor, duty, and inclination, all forbade that I should retract.

"DON'T GO, HANS." I enlisted with Captain X. for three months' service, but the State or government, refused to accept his company for that period; he then arranged to attach his command to the —— Regiment Indiana Volunteers, though there seemed to be some doubt of even it being received; finally he joined the 13th Indiana Infantry, and the company was mustered in on the 28th of April, 1861. Prayers were offered in my behalf in the church at Blankville, and though they may not have done me any good, I am sure they never caused me any harm, and I was always very thankful for them.

We were placed in camps at Summans Station, and there received the necessary drilling to make us fit to shoot and be shot.

The unvarying regularity of bacon as an article of diet soon began to cause dissatisfaction among men who had always been accustomed to considerable variety of food, and the boys, more apt at acquiring the worst features of military life than the best, became proficient foragers before they were half soldiers. The hen roosts of the surrounding country suffered terribly. For a long time I held out manfully against any unlawful appropriation of food, refusing to touch, taste, or handle. I would neither cook or eat the fowls gathered in midnight raids, though daily the sight and smell of fresh, fat, tender, white chickens, roast, broiled, fried and stewed, as brought against or in contrast to the half rancid, strong old bacon, proved a terrible and continual temptation, and one day when the "skippers" in the pig meat issued from the commissary were big enough to get up and bark at one, I fell from grace, and receiving as my share, two out of twelve "appropriated" chickens. I ate the pair at one sitting, and ever after clamored for all I could get.

In order to vary the dull routine of camp life and to obtain funds for extra food and luxuries, we organized a show or entertainment, the performers being men of the regiment. Tickets of admission, 25 cents each, were sold through the country thereabouts, and we had a roaring house. There was every kind of talent, good, bad and indifferent, especially of the two latter grades. I appeared professionally as "The man of Iron," and made my title clear to that high sounding designation by driving pins into my limbs, putting red-hot irons on my tongue for three seconds and other old fashioned tricks.

The show cleared for us over all expenses, thirteen dollars, of which I received twenty-five cents, the boys expending the entire balance for whiskey, as to indulgence in which I was less subject to temptation, and possessed more power of resistance, than in regard to chickens; consequently I did not participate or enjoy any portion of the big drunk, free fighting, damages and splitting headaches that followed the expenditure of our fund "for extra food and luxuries."

Our command was moved to Richmond, Indiana, and it was stated once more that our company was to be transferred to the regiment in which it had first tried to find place; but the change was not effected, and for three years we formed part of the 13th Indiana, led by Colonel Jerry Sullivan.

THE MAN OF IRON.

The captain of my company was a most excellent officer, a veteran of the Mexican war, in which he had lost an arm, as brave a man as ever lived, to whom fear was unknown. We were stationed for instruction at Camp Sullivan, Indianapolis, until July 4th, 1861, when we were transported to Grafton, Va., and there remained for two days while preparing for our first march, which brought us, on the 9th, to the foot of Rich Mountain.

Our uniform at that time consisted of a blue jean suit, the jacket being short and shapeless, and we looked like a lot of overgrown charity-school boys, when without arms and equipments. At one o'clock on the morning of July 11th, with three days' rations in haversacks, our cartridge boxes filled with "buck and ball," and entirely new sensations under our blue jean jackets, the 13th Indiana formed into line knowing that in all human probability there were some who would not answer roll call that night.

We were going to fight. Well, that's what we were there for.

It is no easy thing for even the veteran soldier to prepare calmly for a death struggle in the cold, damp atmosphere and darkness of the hour after midnight. It is an entirely different affair from the hurry, dash, excitement and life of a daylight "fall in" at the long-roll. "There are few men," said the great Napoleon, "possessed of the two o'clock in the morning courage;" and any soldier who has passed through an active campaign will admit the severe strain of such moments ; and now we, almost to be called raw recruits, were mustering in silence under that cold, calm moon, and sparkling stars, to move forward for initiation in scenes of bloody violence.

Our direct commander was General Rosecrans, and after all the battalions had arrived he placed himself at the head of the column ; then came a weary march of thirteen miles over one of the most villanously bad roads that ever tortured foot of man or beast, and we found ourselves in the rear of Rich Mountain, looking up at the frowning batteries erected by the Confederates under General Garnet. Sharp fighting ensued, and I could and would gladly spin a long yarn about that fight, but I am not writing a history of the war, or account of any battles but my own, so I will only say that our side was victorious, and we 13th Indianians came out of our first engagement victorious, and with corresponding proud elation.

A favorite question with non-combatants is : "How did you feel when you were going into and during your first fight ?"

For myself only can I answer and say, that my feeling on the occasion mentioned were mixed and various. Forming into line in the darkness and chill, I was, to a considerable degree "shivery;" I said my prayers with a hearty good will, I went through every prayer that ever I knew, heard, or could invent, and I meant every word I uttered. When we were once before the enemy I own that I felt a little "skeered;" I did not want to be killed or wounded, not even for my country. After the firing began and comrades would now and then drop around me, pity for their fate and prayers for my own safety came into my mind, but soon the work became general and hot, tearing my cartridges I got powder into my mouth, the smoke of battle tingled my nostrils, my mad commenced to rise, I thirsted for revenge, I wanted to get at 'em. I loaded and blazed away with fierce determination to do all the damage I could. By the time the order was given to charge, I had forgotten all about danger and rushed on with the line, full of fight and fury.

And when we charged and drove them ! Ah ! the glory of seeing them flying before us, and feeling to the thrill of victory ! That was absolute, pure, and perfect ecstacy. Our command was actively engaged in that battle for over one hour and the whole time did not seem to me to be ten minutes.

Now you know how I felt in my first battle.

The next day we were to tackle another strong position of the enemy, but that night when we went into camp, I was one of those detailed for picket duty on the outer line. It stormed fearfully all night, and it was a pretty severe lesson to a new soldier to have a long rough march, hard fighting, and picket duty, without overcoat or blanket, and in the hardest kind of rain, all crowded into one twenty-four hours. But the experience did us good.

GIVING IT TO 'EM.

When daylight came our line was formed and we moved upon the enemy, observing, of course, all proper precautions. To our surprise there were no returns of our opening shots, and in a short time we discovered that the foe had decamped during the darkness, taking with them their ammunition and arms, but leaving behind all their baggage, camp equipage and rations.

The retreating forces was one of the crack Southern organizations, that early in the war was composed of men of wealth, and they were splendidly provided with everything that money could purchase. These South Carolina cadets had been obliged to leave behind them a profusion of luxurious appointings, fine clothing, dainties in food and liquors, royal cigars, canned fruits and meats, everything in fact that two years later the poor, gallant fellows, and all belonging to them had almost forgotten the use or taste of.

The letters we found from the sweethearts, wives and families to those who were in the field were one and all filled with expressions and sentiments of such devotion to "The

PICKET—NOT PIC-NIC.

Cause," that it was easy to understand the influences which so intensely "fired the Southern heart."

CHAPTER XV.

OF BATTLES, BULLETS, BAYONETS AND BLOOD.

Our regiment's next station was at Beverly, Va.; from there we moved to Hutchinville and then to Elkwater, where our duty was mostly marching back and forth to Cheat Mountain, though there were small skirmishes constantly occurring to keep one's blood from stagnating.

At Hutchinville I was taken ill with what seemed to me a complication and conglomeration of all the diseases incident to camp life, and all the ills that flesh is heir to and on the face of the earth I don't think at that time, there was a more miserable poor fellow than myself.

I was blessed with a good hearted comrade, named Frank McCoy; he went out one day and rooted around until he gathered a double handful of boneset and made it into the strongest tea possible ; I put in my whole week's ration of sugar to sweeten it, but it still was strong and bitter enough to raise a blister on a side of sole leather, and I drank it.

Shortly after I had put the terrible concoction inside of me, the long roll was sounded in our camp, the rattle of small arms was heard at the front, and it was evident that a very brisk little fight was going on.

I was sure, two seconds before hearing all this, that I could not have moved a yard to save me, but when these sounds saluted my ears, I seized my musket, and dragged myself or crawled over the ground to where our line was formed. The excitement, exertion, or boneset, or all three of them, threw me into a profuse perspiration, and restored the healthy action of my system so that in three or four days I reported as fit for duty.

The summer campaign was rather lacking in stirring incidents, but during October we were started out to Hollow Fork to gun for guerrillas. By orders we were supplied with three days' rations, but as we were out just three times three days, in a country where there was little or nothing to forage, we were very nearly starved ; we did get some corn meal, which we made into mush, but as we had no salt, it was very poor grub indeed.

At one time I thought I had struck a bonanza ; at an old man's house was discovered a hidden barrel of bear meat, and the boys made short work of it; I started for my share among the last and had secured a good big piece, when our captain, who had heard of the proceedings, made his appearance. He put his pistol almost in my face and told me that if I didn't drop that bear meat, he'd .*drop* me ; he would have done it in a moment, and I knew it. I dropped the meat.

By the time we returned to camp from that scout, the miserable, shoddy leather shoes furnished the soldiers, were worn completely off the feet of myself and many others, and we marched over miles and miles of rough, frozen and snow covered roads, leaving the blood tracks of our naked, cut and bruised feet to mark our trail.

DROP IT.

We were next ordered to cut logs and build huts in preparation for going into winter quarters. Hardly had we completed our rough houses when we were marched off to Beverly, from whence, on December 11th, there started a battalion composed of ten men from each company of four regiments to make an attack on a body of the enemy, entrenched on the summit of the Allegheny mountains, fifty miles distant. In the detachment from my regiment I had the honor to be one.

We reached the stronghold of the foe on the 13th, and at once engaged them. For three hours our force fought desperately and did all that men could do to win, but our opponents held an impregnable position, and after we had lost nearly one hundred and fifty men, our lines began to weaken, and when the fresh and brave Johnnies charged out from behind their works and "went for us" with a will, our boys became the most demoralized crowd I ever got into, and every fellow at once started to the rear "to reorganize."

The retreat at the first start of it took the form of a scattering foot race, every man for himself, etc. etc., and as for my part in the procession

after it turned tail I run. I had stood up to my work and fought like a man while all the others did, but when the panic set in, I caught the complaint bad, and when the movement to the rear began to assume the nature of a foot race I made up my mind, all of it, and in a hurry; that I was going to come out ahead if trying would do it, and I ran as I never had before until I arrived at Beverly.

It had taken 27 hours for our command to reach the fighting ground; I made the return trip "double quick" in less than half that time. If unable to boast of my great achievement in battle on that occasion I can at least brag of my record in the go-as-you-please foot race that followed.

TO THE REAR—"TO RE-ORGANIZE."

In a short time after this inglorious affair we were moved to Cumberland, as railroad guards on the Baltimore and Ohio line, and several jolly little skirmishes served to keep us alive and active, especially one at Sir John's Run. The opening of 1862, found us encamped at Pawpaw Tunnel, under command of General F. W. Lander, who there died on March 2d, very suddenly, while preparing to resist a midnight attack on our station; a true patriot and gallant a soldier as ever fought for the flag was this noble man.

General James Shields then took command and under the veteran of Mexico's fame, we took part in the fight at Winchester, which commenced on the evening of March 22d, when we repulsed a force of the enemy under General Ashby.

We were busy all that night with preparations for the contest, sure to come in the morning. Very early on the 23d, a small Confederate force appeared before us; it was evident that the Johnnies were "laying low," but our artillery opening upon their position soon unmasked them; out they came and a square fight, of the hammer and tongs order ensued, during which, by an attack on the left flank of the enemy, we got them where we wanted them for a general attack, which was made at five o'clock in the afternoon with great success, we capturing guns, small arms and prisoners in large lots. General Shields was wounded in the arm and we lost many men, the 81st and 110th Pennsylvania regiments catching it particularly hot. I was detailed with a party after the fight to hunt up and carry off the field the wounded men ; our colonel was with us for a time, and as we were moving about, some poor chap cried out that he had his leg broken, to come and help him, to which appeal the colonel replied :

"Shut up your noise over a little thing like that, here's a poor fellow with the whole top of his head off, and he don't utter a groan."

The morning after our battle we marched to New Market, where we captured many stragglers. Then followed a season of activity ; marching over Luray Valley to Port Royal and other places, picket duty and small engagements.

One day I crossed the Luray river with a portion of my company, to "feel the enemy." Instead of waiting for us, they came before we expected them and made us feel them in a manner decidedly unpleasant. By some blunder our party was caught between cross-fires and a scratch gravel change of base was the only way out of the fix. I ran away again, as fast and far as I could, being brought to a dead halt by reaching the banks of a river. I had then the choice of dying by water through drowning, or giving up the ghost through fire of the pursuing enemy. But I did not desire to die at all.

Fortune sent me a preserver in the shape of a badly scared cavalry man who was urging his horse to the utmost. I begged his aid and he took charge of my musket while I seized hold of the horse's tail and was towed through the stream to safety on the opposite side. I have noted this incident as it gives me opportunity to remark that it was my most (horse) hair-breadth escape of the war.

A (HORSE) HAIR BREADTH ESCAPE.

We were taken by rail to Alexandria, and there took transports to Harrison's Landing, where we arrived July 2d, just in time to cover the retreat of McClellan from Malvern Hill.

At Harrison's Landing, little was done but parade, drill and build fortifications. It was while stationed here that, one day on picket duty, I blundered in attempting to jump over a ditch, and fell inside instead, sustaining an injury (Hernia), which proved most serious in its results.

I was treated in camp and afterwards sent to Hampton Hospital at Fortress Monroe, where I remained until, after due inspection and investigation, I was pronounced by the U. S. Medical Authorities to be incurable, and was therefor honorably discharged from the military service in October, 1862—another singular coincidence, all my U. S. discharges having been given in that month of the year.

CHAPTER XVI.
TO DENMARK AND BACK.

During all my soldier life, I had, from time to time, sent to my good friend and former employer, Mr. Stuart, a portion of my pay, and he now held in trust for me the sum of sixty dollars.

I felt a strong inclination to start for Blankville at once, bright-eyed Miss Maggie being the most powerful magnet in that direction; for not only did pleasant recollections of the past continually enter my mind, but there was the tempting future to contemplate, and distance lent additional enchantment to the view; I longed to learn if the hopes I fondly cherished could ever arrive at happy fruition.

But I well knew that, with the small amount of money at my command, I could do nothing as a farmer, unless I again engaged as a laborer, and this did not suit my ideas; I was becoming more ambitious in regard to situation in life, so I restrained my powerful desire to take the first train for Indiana, and resolved to obey an equally ardent impulse which I had long been trying to keep under control.

The truth of the matter was, for months I had been under a fit of the "homesicks"; for years, ever since I had left my mother, I had earnestly longed to once more see her, though my circumstances had never been, for any extended time, sufficiently prosperous to warrant me in acting in accordance with the promptings of my heart. I felt now as though I had earned the right to enjoy a rest and holiday, and I decided to go back to Denmark and astonish my mother, brothers and sisters.

Having positively resolved upon the trip, I next formed myself into a committee of the whole on ways and means. I wished to save every cent that I could, in order that I might make some show of means, liberality and responsibility before and with my family and acquaintances. Not to spend a single unnecessary cent was my great object until my arrival in my native land, and I resorted to every honorable expedient to save the pennies.

"DOT PEUDIVUL VOTCH."

At Buffalo, as I was returning from the army, I met a party of drovers and by assisting them in taking care of their cattle, I earned a free passage to New York. In that city I equipped myself for the proposed journey, purchasing a good outfit of well made clothing in Broadway.

A silver watch also I bought on the Bowery, from a gentleman whose features very plainly indicated his religious belief, and whose profuse recommendations of the excellence of the "ticker" were fully born out in its subsequent performances. I was determined that my mother and others should see that the "stupid dunder head" of the family did not return, after his many years of wandering in the fashion and fix of the Biblical Prodigal Son. Even though I had been brought mighty low down in my time, and even very glad at one time to sleep with a pig, I was not fool enough to return with the husks and the wallow clinging to me and go grunting about to prove the truth of the old gossips who had once vowed that I "would come to be hanged."

In planning or seeking economical methods of transportation, I was fortunate enough to discover that by serving as dish-washer or scullion on board a Hamburg steamer I could obtain a free passage across. I applied for and obtained such a situation and made the trip in that capacity.

The vessel touched at several points before reaching Hamburg and I was anxious to leave it at a point from which I could most quickly reach those from whom I had been so long parted. I was told that if I quitted the ship before she finished the voyage I would receive no pay for my services. I had not expected anything but free passage and though I would much liked to have had the money, yet now I was near my family I could not restrain my impatience, so I went ashore at the quarantine stoppage and made quick time for my old home, thus sacrificing my wages. And soon I wished I had curbed my desires and taken in the cash.

At last I was at my mother's ; neither she nor my brothers recognized

me, but a few words and moments cleared away all the clouds that years had formed before their eyes and my welcome was as hearty as the most exacting affection could desire.

I was given the freedom of the town in a social sense, and I did not spare the contents of my purse in returning the hospitality showered upon me by my family, friends and neighbors. Everybody now protested that they had always seen "the making of a fine and successful man in me." In fact, I was rather too profuse in expenditure, and, as I saw my cash

"DON'T YOU KNOW ME ?"

melting away like snow before a summer sun, I said unto myself, in choice American slang, "My son, its time for you to git up and git."

To save the humiliation of confessing that I had exhausted my means, I made excuse that my permit to remain in the country would soon expire; this was the truth, but not the whole truth. I had left but one $5 bill ; it would take all of that to land me in Hamburg, and once there I would be obliged to trust to luck to obtain passage back to the United States.

Bidding a most affectionate farewell to relatives and friends, I started forward to meet and grapple with my troubles. When I reached Hamburg, I made my home at a very second rate boarding house and most diligently sought to ship on some vessel and earn my passage over the Atlantic. But my earnest efforts met with no success, and I was very soon destitute.

While studying to find a way out of my difficulties, I suddenly remembered the great admiration my eldest brother had expressed of my watch. I could think of no other way to extricate myself but by sacrificing my pride and the "ticker" at the same time, so I wrote to brother, confessed my poverty, and told him that if he would send me money equivalent to

$7.50 of Uncle Sam's cash, I would forward him the time-piece by mail. He complied with my request, and I purchased with his remittance a ticket on a steamer to South Hampton, England, which was as far as the amount would pay my way.

I had taken this action in the hope that Providence or luck would assist me at South Hampton, in finding some means of getting to America. Before we reached my stopping point, I heard that one of the coal heavers on the vessel had been so crippled as to be incapacitated for work so I at once made application and was installed in his place, being thus enabled to keep on with my journey.

With the hardest kind of hard labor I paid for my transportation in that ship, for she had been injured by collision with icebergs on the coast of New Foundland, and was in a very leaky condition; so leaky, that we who had to shovel coal were obliged to stand over knee deep in foul smelling, slimy, black bilge water all the time we were at work.

Through fire and water we contrived to make our way safely, and in March, 1863, I again landed in New York so completely "dead broke," that I was forced to sell my pocket comb to an American citizen of African descent (who had no earthly use for it, in his black wool), for the small sum of three cents wherewith to pay my passage on the ferry boat over into New Jersey.

Once in the State of sand and mosquitoes I made a bee line for the plank road that leads to Newark and took up my march in that direction. The only person who responded to my appeals for work and food was a market gardener who offered me a chance to gain plenty of the former and little of the latter, and with him I engaged.

By this time my clothing was in a most dilapidated condition, the wind went whistling through every portion of my tattered raiment as freely as water will run through a sieve; the blighting March breezes played hide and seek in and under my fluttering rags and seemed to blow through and through and

MIGHTY HARD UP.

freeze my flesh, blood, bones and marrow.

Verily, it was a cool reception I met on returning to the land of my adoption.

CHAPTER XVII.
MORE VARIATIONS ON THE OLD TUNE.

I had tried to sustain with dignity my character as a "self-made man" during my visit to Denmark, now I found myself a self-unmade individual in the land of liberty, equality and fraternity, where "one man's as good as another, and often a deal better;" where "any smart young fellow must get along and grow rich;" all of which facts or fictions I had spouted out and insisted upon to my Danish audiences, when, well clothed, with money to spend, a watch chain to play with, I had posed as an illustration of the prosperity which could be acquired by "any smart young fellow" in the great and glorious Star Spangled Union.

Here I now was, in land of the free and home of the brave, on an equality with vagrants of the lowest class, toiling, hard as ever did any black slave; with half clothed shivering anatomy and toil racked bones on a Jersey truck patch, just keeping body and life together on the crumbs that fell from the miserly table of my master; Lazarus was a millionaire in comparison to me. This was the role I was now filling after a brilliant starring tour abroad.

My work on the truck patch was to dig out of the frozen ground the root vegetables, carrots, etc., etc., to wash them in icy water, and get them ready for city market. The generous master had furnished me a blanket about as thick, warm and holy as a fish net, and I was kindly permitted to sleep in the barn along with the other half fed animals.

In this man's service I slaved and starved, froze and famished for seven days; then I could stand it no longer; I could certainly do no worse and would very likely do much better out on the tramp, and out on the tramp I determined to go. When I informed the root grubber of my intended departure, he only remarked that "it's all right, you ain't no 'count anyway," and he took advantage of my voluntary retirement by refusing to pay me any wages, claiming that I had contracted to stay a month.

Once more on the road without a cent, the necessity was forced upon me of resorting to my old tactics as a tramp, and well did these serve me at my first call upon them. I made application at a house for dinner, and was shortly told that they had no food cooked and were not likely to have for an indefinite period. But I was very, very hollow inside, and so I thought I would try and see what blarney would do to furnish up my empty bread basket.

"Oh, miss!" said I, to the sour-faced vixen who was turning away, "never mind the grub, I'll worry along somehow, but do just let me tell your fortune, I see it in your bright eyes and pretty face. I can tell any one's fortune the moment I see them, it's a natural gift I have, my family is all that way."

"Oh, you get out!" said she, stopping and decidedly molified, "I don't believe in no sich nonsense."

"Now just look here, my dear young lady," put in I, quickly, "listen to me for just three minutes, and then if you don't own up that I'm a hocus pocus, seventh son of a seventh son, you can call the dog and I'll let him make a light lunch on what little meat there is left on my bones. My mother was a real genuine gypsy queen right from Egypt, and each of her children has to travel and beg food for seven years before they are given

73

their fortune ; my pilgrimage will be over next month, and if I don't starve to death before then, I will be worth millions."

"Oh, git out!" again said the woman, though evidently puzzled and curious, "what do I care for all your stuff and gibberish!"

"Just wait one moment, Miss, just one moment!" I exclaimed, and partly closing my eyes and motioning with my hands, I slowly muttered:

"I see, I see, a young man with dark hair, and a pretty girl ; why, it's you; and there is a church, and a minister waiting for a wedding, and, there is something—a woman—comes in between the girl and the man—now she comes on and now she goes off—I never can see futures well in the open air—I could see her face plain if I was in a room."

All this time I was slyly watching the foolish face and could see that I had struck on something so near the truth that it would pass muster for that article, so I opened my eyes and returned her stare of amazement with a look of confidence.

"How's that?" I asked, "Aint that getting the seventh son business down pretty fine?"

"Why, why ; how did you know?" she slowly said, and then, "come round to the kitchen door."

THE "SEVENTH SON" BUSINESS.

I went around to and in through the kitchen door ; with that female I "made myself solid," and I revictualed my stowage compartment until I could pack away no more, then I departed promising to see her later and to reveal all the future had in store for her.

I havn't been back yet, though.

That night was a fearfully stormy time ; in the words of the poet, "fust it blew, an' then it snew, an' then begun to friz," and I struck for the railroad track, jumped the first freight train that came along, fortunately escaped detection as I clung, cold, wet and miserable, huddled up on the bumper between two cars, until I was carried to Camden, N. J.

I had left from my European trip a pocket knife that cost two shillings; this I sold for a few pennies and paid my ferriage over to Philadelphia, there I went at once to the good friend, Gottleib, who had before received me, when in an equally bad fix, and he again gave me warm welcome, feeding and lodging me gratis. As he knew it would be impossible for me to obtain employment in the scare-crow condition of my clothing, the whole of which would hardly have made a wad for a big gun, he fixed me up decently in attire, and for fourteen days I hunted in every quarter of that city for work and wages.

THE "TROTTER CASES."

Fearing that even if I did not wear out my welcome I would be too much of a tax upon the limited means of my generous friend, I told him that it was useless to remain in Philadelphia, and if he would furnish me a pair of shoes I would once more try fortune in the West. He promptly provided the "trotter cases" and I started off.

After seven days' travel, I brought up again in Blankville, Blanklin Co., Indiana. My reception by the Stuart family was as kind as I could wish, though my heart was saddened by the very evident change plainly

noticeable in the manner my cherished one responded my demonstrations. I had pursuaded myself that I had a very strong hold upon her affections, but it was soon made perfectly clear, most unmistakably certain to my very unwilling mind that no trace of tenderness for me now existed in her heart, while a good stout lump of the same was there for somebody else.

I soon fell into the old routine about the place of Mr. Stuart, and turned my hand to a multitude of odd jobs ; but the keen, constant interest in everything I said or did, which had been manifested by the family when I previously lived there, was now wanting ; during my absence other persons and affairs had replaced me in the front rank of their life, and "WHERE ARE NOW THE HOPES I CHERISHED ?" while they were as kind and pleasant as it was possible to be, yet there was that wanting without which it was no home of contentment for me.

In a few days, I told the Stuart family that I should go to Chicago and try to obtain work there, so with many good wishes from all, I started for that city, and on arrival started out after employment, meeting with no success, being rejected on account of my disability, when I tried to re-enlist in the army, and getting very hard up.

Hardly expecting to succeed, I presented myself as a recruit for the naval service. Of course the injury which caused my discharge and kept me out from the army was discovered when examined by the medical officer, but when he reported the fact to the shipping master, a veteran captain, that good natured soul said, "Oh, pass him anyhow, he's an old salt and worth a dozen green horns." So I passed and once more wore the navy blue.

THE CAPTAIN, GUN, AND CREW.

This time I was destined to be a fresh water sailor. With a squad of other tars, I was sent to Cairo, Ill., and put on the gun boat CONESTOGA, Thomas Selfridge, commander, but on this vessel I remained for a very short time, being transferred to gun boat No. 13, FORT HINEMAN, Captain Pierce.

It was not long before I was made captain of a gun, and

awarded other positions as rewards of merit, which I filled creditably and retained until, in an unlucky moment, it was discovered that I was an artist in the culinary preparation of beans; that I could cook beans without burning them. What sad memories were recalled as I reflected upon the miseries through which I passed while acquiring such skill.

I was promoted from captain of a gun to be assistant cook, and my great talents were so evident and so highly appreciated that, in a little while I was made chief of the galley, with the extra pay and all allowances, privileges, etc., to which that important functionary is through law and custom fully entitled.

PROMOTED.

The duty of our vessel was to act as picket guard along the Mississippi, and take our share in such general fighting as we could pick up.

We were at Vicksburg on that memorable 4th of July, when General U. S. Grant gobbled Pemberton and his army, and the next day we lay off Port Hudson, while a like ceremony was being enacted within its line of fortifications.

At Ellis' Cliff below Natchez, Miss., we took a turn at river guard duty, and then our boat formed part of the equipment of General N. P. Banks when, in his unfortunate Red River expedition, he acted as quartermaster for the Confederate forces in that section, by allowing them to scoop up all the army and private supplies and baggage of his division.

We were one of the fleet of Admiral Porter, at Alexandria, La., when the Rebs tried to leave our boats stuck in the mud by drawing the water from the river. The practical knowledge and skill of a western ex-lumber man, Lieut. Col. Bailey, acting engineer of the 19th army corps, enabled us to escape by the construction of a dam, such as is used to "boom" logs through the western rivers, and through such means saved the entire fleet.

During this time we had many fights with the enemy posted behind shore batteries. One of these engagements was a decidedly hot affair, and we were raked and riddled in a most effective manner. This was near Fort De Russy; we had on board our craft beside our own men, the crew of the gun boat EASTPORT, which had been sunk by a torpedo, and of the combined crews in the fight mentioned, over fifty were killed and a large number wounded.

At the gun over which I served as captain, a Parrot cannon of the largest size, there were eleven men killed out of the twenty-two who manned it. The deck had to be continually

HOT WORK AT FORT DE RUSSY.

fresh sanded, so slippery did it become from the excessive and constant flow of blood. The boilers and machinery of the boat had cotton bales piled around for protection, but the hot fire soon ignited this, and we were obliged to throw it overboard ; our vessel was hulled thirteen times by cannon balls, peppered completely by musket shots and so crippled, that we were forced to withdraw from action and make our way slowly, like a big floating hearse, to Alexandria.

I still retain a most vivid recollection of that fight.

CHAPTER XVIII.
NEW TRAILS, TRIALS AND TRIBULATIONS.

While in the section referred to in the last chapter, we captured in a Bayou two Confederate steamboats, loaded with several thousand bales of cotton, a commodity then worth a high price in our own and the English markets.

These prizes made our hearts jubilant, all hands and the cook being busy figuring up the probable amount of prize money they would receive, and the fun they would have in spending it.

But there is a saying in the navy that prize money is strained, for its distribution, through a ladder; that the officers get all dropping through, and Jack receives only what lodges on the rounds. My share of our rich booty was exactly fifteen dollars; there may have been more due and assigned me, but that is the entire sum I received from the agent who collected my claim.

On the eighth day of July, 1864; after serving one year and eight days, I was again honorably discharged from the naval service, and took passage up the river for Cairo, Ill.

On the way, our boat was fired into by a party of guerrillas on the shore, a favorite practice of those outlaws. It might be supposed that I, having "been through the mill," in both army and navy, was calmly indifferent to these demonstrations. Nothing of the kind; I argued to myself that, being now out of service, if I got killed it would be of no benefit to the country or myself; if I was wounded, I would not be pensioned and the doctor's bill would come out of my pocket, and so I hunted the spot on that boat where in my judgment a bullet was least likely to find its way, and there I stowed myself and kept so stowed until all danger was passed.

The barbarous habit of firing on unarmed boats was kept on this river until the gangs poured a volley into the little steamer MITTEE STEVENS, when she was going to Red River with a lot of captured Confederate officers to be exchanged; there were a number of these killed, and then active measures were taken to put a stop to the murderous proceeding.

At Cairo I was paid off, and with several hundred dollars in hand I proceeded to New York, where I purchased a steerage passage in a steamer for Aspinwall, paying therefore two hundred dollars, my objective point being San Francisco, California.

Upon arrival at Aspinwall, with others I started across the Isthmus of Panama, halting on our way at Acapulco, so that we did not reach San Francisco until August 4th, 1864.

After unsuccessful search for employment in the city, I found work at the salt works, near Mount Eaton, thirty miles up the bay from 'Frisco, and here I did well so long as I stuck to work I could do and made no attempt to branch out.

But one day the old luck instigated me to try my hand at taking the place of engineer, to run a little dummy engine used to haul trucks loaded with salt over a wooden railroad. I brought the machine to a halt by putting too heavy a load on the cars, then in starting again I managed to get my left foot under the wheels, which passed directly over and left it mashed flat as a pancake, and that settled my business completely.

There was neither comfortable accommodations or medical attendance to be obtained at the Salt Mines, so the next day I was bundled into the stage and taken back to San Francisco, where, boarding being expensive, and the doctors' charges high, my cash account soon began to present a most discouraged and weary aspect, and in a spirit of self-preservation, I hobbled to its portals in search of comfort and admission in the City Hospital, where I was received and remained until cured.

It was the old, old story repeated, when once again I could use my feet, and use them I did, tramping through the streets hunting for work and finding none.

After many days of ill success, I at last found a boss, a rather "off-color" man and brother he was, and his occupation was the manufacture of soap.

John Dyer had no prejudice against me because I was about ten shades whiter in skin than himself; he considered "a white man was just as good as a nigger, so long as he behaved himself decent," and he gave me work at which I stuck and (excuse the word) stunk for about two months."

CRIPPLED IN FOOT AND FINANCES.

A combined attack of the rambling and the war fevers then took hold of my brain and bones, the large bounties offered to all men who would join the Second California regiment, then being organized, tended to greatly aggravate the disease, and finally contriving to pass muster without rejection by the surgeon, I buttoned for the second time about my body the blue and brass and came to a "shoulder arms."

For nine months our command lay in Presidio, near Fort Point; while there we received the news of the assassination of President Lincoln, our feelings when told of this horror can be easily imagined.

The first move of the regiment was to Wilmington, about twenty miles from Los Angeles, near Drum Barracks, then over the great sandy desert, we marched to Fort Yuma,

AN "OFF-COLOR" BOSS.

stopping for a few days of rest in the bottom lands of Colorado, under the shadow of the Hill of Fort Yuma.

Then away again along the Gila River and through the rocky desert, to and past Oatman's Flat, the bloody spot where an unfortunate family of that name were inhumanly tortured and butchered by the Indians.

Off again, over and through the great 56 miles of desert plain, destitute of everything but mesquite trees, cactus, tarantulas and rattlesnakes ; marching ever on, no resting place of grateful shade to cheer us, toiling over mile after mile to Maricopa Wells, and then one more day's tramping brought us to Whilesville.

This last named place is also known as Pima Village, and is a town inhabited by the Acabulta Tribe of Indians, who still retain the primitive manners and customs of their forefathers, but cultivate the soil and carry the wheat they raise to the mill.

One unalterable Mede and Persian law exists among this people; any departure from chastity by a female of that tribe is punished with death; they keep a keen and continual watch, and the penalty invariably quickly follows detection.

A striking illustration that Indian savageness was by no means crushed

out or subdued in this tribe, was afforded us by the sight of a dried body of an Apache warrior, which was hanging to or swinging from the limb of a tree, and was kept there to serve as a target and aid to the aboriginal schoolmaster in teaching the young Injun idea how to shoot. The dessicated subject seemed to have served a long term in his then position, or the arrow proficiency of the young redskins was wonderfully good, for the carcass of that warrior fairly bristled with barbs, sticking out at all points, in all directions, like "quills upon a fretful porcupine."

Continuing our march we arrived at Fort Breckenridge, now Camp Grant, where we built huts, and there was established our headquarters.

From Camp Grant we were sent out on several expeditions against marauding Indians ; a notable though short campaign of this kind being that of the ascent of the Arrow Wiper

A SUBJECT FULL OF FINE POINTS. Canyon, on which occasion our Colonel, George Wright, was guilty of, or attempted to execute an atrocity, which was a disgrace to civilization and an outrage on humanity.

When we came within sight of the Indians for whom we were hunting our commanding officer ordered a white flag, a flag of truce, to be displayed, and the pursued people waited our coming in perfect confidence of their safety, for even an Indian understands and respects that signal of peace.

As we moved up, the Colonel divided and disposed of his force in such a manner as would, or he thought it would entirely surround the poor creatures and cut off every means of escape, and then, to the astonishment of every human being on both sides, he gave orders for immediate and rapid firing.

As soldiers, we were bound to obey orders, and we blazed away. The Indians disappeared as though the ground had swallowed them up; where

they went, or how much they suffered from our firing I know not, but I do know that neither I or any of my comrades ever saw a dead Indian out of that lot, and if any of my own shots killed one of them, he must have been high up in the air, for in that direction were all my bullets sent, and I believe every man of the party acted in the same way.

Our entire rank and file were excited and indignant at the inhuman and unsoldierly act of the Colonel, and many of our men paid a terrible price

HIGH AIMS.

in return for his treachery, an invisible foe hung upon our flanks day and night, dropping our boys right and left. Woe to any poor fellow who straggled from our line, he was

caught and tortured to death with all the refinement of savage cruelty, and the remains of his horribly mutilated body left as a warning to others. For the blood of every man thus slain, Colonel Wright was directly responsible.

On our return to camp from this ill-fated scout, my irrepressible propensity to get myself into trouble, caused me to inaugurate a private war of my own, which resulted in my back having to suffer for the offences of my tongue.

We had been living on short rations for considerable time, owing to much of the meat being so spoiled as to be unfit for consumption. Now officers receive money in lieu of the ration furnished the men, and they should and are in honor bound to subsist on provisions bought by themselves,. but our Captain, Chauncy Fairchild by name, but fair in no other particle, made it a

INDIAN VENGEANCE.

habit to take his supplies from those issued to the soldiers.

To feed one man out of stores intended for fifty, takes a very small amount from each one of that party, but it is a very small business for an officer to engage in, and I was bound to protest against it, so I opened my mouth, and in language more plain than polite, more expressive than elegant, I gave vent to my opinion in regard to the Captain's meanness and dishonesty; and all that I said was duly and fully reported to him by one of his todies.

Very promptly and pointedly were charges and specifications made out against me. A court martial was convened, and in less than no time a verdict of "Guilty" as to "conduct prejudicial to good order and military discipline" was recorded against my name. The sentence condemned me

to thirty days' hard labor about the camp, and confinement at night in the guard house, where there were two filthy Indian prisoners who were very much alive—also their blankets.

My condemnation was duly carried out and served through, the dignity of my superior officer was upheld, discipline properly inculcated, outraged regulations vindicated, and the Captain allowed without hindrance to steal the rations of his men.

COMPANIONS IN MISERY.

CHAPTER XIX.
OUT OF THE BLUE AND INTO BUSINESS.

Soon after I had served my sentence and been restored to duty, the regiment was relieved from duty at that post by the 14th United States Infantry, one of the new regiments of "Regulars" raised by Act of Congress after the war.

The 14th United States Infantry was at that time, without exception,

the most perfect collection of thieves, cowards, cut-throats, drunkards, gutter snipes and "Whiskey Bums" of every degree, that ever escaped universal and well deserved hanging, and were allowed, for some all wise reason to infest the tops of the earth. Their present assignment came nearer to their proper sphere than any spot could be found until after their individual deaths.

Our own men were not, by any means, a set of saints, but the very worst rip in our command was a white robed angel of heavenly grace, compared with the best

FEATURES FROM THE FEAR-specimen that could have been selected
FUL 14TH.   among the scum of scum of creation that was gathered into the ranks of the 14th Regulars, and very gladly we marched away from the most miserable locality that ever tormented poor soldiers, and left behind us the meat for gallows of our army.

With only one or two deviations we followed the same route as on our outward march when returning to our former headquarters. I had an opportunity to learn something of the remarkable dryness of the atmosphere and absence of rain which marks that section; after leaving that place I missed from my kit a large knife which I had just before purchased; on our return there I hunted about the place where I had last been using it, and I discovered it sticking just where I had left it, without a stain of rust or soil upon it, bright as a new dollar.

When we arrived at Anaheim, twelve miles from Wilmington, the men of our regiment began to sell everything for which they could find a purchaser, their arms, the camp and garrison equipage, anything and everything that would bring in money was bartered for it and the proceeds expended for rum, on which there was a big drunk of two days' duration, in which I am happy to say, I in no way participated.

We reached Wilmington at last, and there embarked for San Francisco, and reached that city in time to be mustered out on May 10th, 1866.

The sum total of my savings, bounty and final big pay reached about $400, and I concluded to carry out an idea I had conceived; to start off to and through Oregon Territory on a peddling venture.

I had heard so much of the "web-foots" that I had an intense desire to make a close acquaintance with, and as many dollars as possible off, the good natured Oregonians.

With the firm of Tobias and Davidson I invested over three-fourths of my capital, buying cheap, glittering trinkets and ornaments, with about an ounce of gold to a ton of brass, but manufactured, and of a character, to find a ready sale among the class of people with whom I was about to come in contact, then I bought a ticket for Portland city, and from there started out to open my new campaign.

On my journey to Portland I made the acquaintance of a young doctor, Slagimdote, I will here call him; and the intimacy I contracted with him exercised a very considerable influence on my future life, as will be seen hereafter.

The doctor and myself went to board at the same hotel, and as he most assiduously cultivated my good opinion, and I had not the least suspicion of, nor did he allow me to see his true character, we were soon fast friends; and on my side, at least, the kindly feeling was sincere and entirely disinterested. I had procured a box, specially made for easy carriage, and from the trunk containing all my stock, I packed this with an assortment and started off up the Willamet Valley in search of customers and profit.

My adventures on this trip were all of the most pleasant nature; the valley is a garden spot of the earth, well sprinkled with as pretty, lively, healthy daughters of Mother Eve as can be found anywhere.

Most of the men folks being absent at the mines, it was something of an event when there arrived in the midst of these jolly maidens a young man who was willing, and whose business it was to flatter them to the top of their bent and make himself as agreeable as possible.

The contents of my box added to my own attractions and fascinations, caused a flutter of excitement equal to the advent of a circus in a country town, and the glittering trinkets dazzled their eyes, and the soft accents of Danish-English blarney tickled their ears.

I could and did court a new girl every night, always of course in a perfectly respectful way, the guardian mothers and fear of fathers and big brothers with handy shot guns insuring that; and I lived in clover. I could have, and I might have done worse, selected from dozens who were ready to enter into life partnership with me, and many times I was forced to listen to Mam, when I would have far preferred "buzzing" Sis; while the dame advised me that I should marry and settle down, and then proceeded to dilate upon the many and manifold accomplishments, virtues and housewifely excellences of the bright-eyed daughter.

They would delicately express their confidence in me, hint how Sis was "took" after me, what a fine, stout handsome pair we would make; there was just such a spot where, with a store, mill, or tavern we could make our everlasting fortune, Sis and me, and continue in such strain until I was all blushes, confusion and talk-tired.

The life I was now leading was full of enjoyment for me. I was passing through an immense and beautiful garden, meeting free spoken, bright handsome girls and sharpening my wits, in which I had learned to put considerable confidence, by friction with all kinds of antagonists. That I sometimes met with keener ones I had several proofs. At

FASCINATIONS.

the city of Salem, bartering with the dashing factory lasses, I was several times the victim of "put up" jobs, and while one of the sparkling little rogues attracted my attention, another would secure some coveted article of my stock without troubling me to name the price or make change in payment. But such matters could easily be put down to profit and loss account, and the profit side could stand it. But this is a digression.

At every farm house or comfortable dwelling I offered and pushed my goods with the persistence necessary to the successful prosecution of my trade. The wares a peddler has to dispose of are secondary considerations; cheek, gab and good nature are the commodities he requires in unlimited quantities, and I added to my stock in that line each day of my life and experience.

By the female portion of the community my coming was always

PROFIT AND LOSS.

met with a hearty welcome, and the inspection, comparison, gossip and purchasing, the latter invariably preceded by long, cunningly conducted "jewing down" was a happy event and grand break in the monotony of their unvarying routine lives, it being only by rare chance and through travellers that they are ever afforded a chance to gain a glimpse of the outside world.

The men of that region, I regret to state, did not appreciate my missionary efforts for the introduction of refined adornments. When I did happen to find them at home, there was lacking in their reception of myself and pack, that outburst of "come in and sit down," which marked the greeting of the lady inhabitants. Masculinity seemed to be more inclined to and liberal in offering, orders to vacate and bites from the dog than with dollars and dimes. They, the men, fully understood that if I once gained hearing of their wives and daughters, and could for a moment flash my glittering breast-pins, ear-rings and bracelets before their eyes, away would go, in my pockets, some considerable amount of their hard earned cash.

The elderly and more settled ladies would sometimes attempt to resist being led in temptation, and "wanted nothing in my line to-day;" or warned me to "pass on—no time to spare," they would say; but a judicious administration of a dose of "taffy" and the exhibition of my samples would, in nine cases out of ten, result in examination, inclination to purchase, and finally, sale.

THEY HAD "NO USE" FOR EAR-RINGS. Good nature breeds good nature, and that "molasses catches more flies than vinegar," is a truism that should be a point of cardinal doctrine with every young man who wishes to make his way successfully through the world.

Politeness costs nothing, and generally pays large dividends on small investments, is a fact that ought to be noted in the mental memorandum of every one.

But I am writing facts and history, not sermons, and it is time I grappled with a new chapter in my life as a peddler.

CHAPTER XX.
THE PECULIARITIES AND PHILOSOPHY OF PEDDLING.

In pursuit of prosperity, in connection with my advocation as a peddler, I fashioned my manner and means much on the pattern of that amusing old rascal, *Autolycus*, introduced by Shakespeare in his "Winter's Tale." This similarity occurred without intention on my part, or knowledge of my distinguished prototype; but I had quickly discerned that the average human would much rather trade with a merry hearted sinner than a grim visaged, grum, scanty speeched saint. So I tried always to be in a happy humor.

"Here!" I would say, "here are ribbons and threads, bright as your eyes, strong and lasting as your affections; razors and knives, sharp as your wits; buttons, to hold you in; and head dresses to set you off; combs that will work the ideas of new fixings for you into the heads of your husbands; brushes that pull out every gray hair from your curls; chains, charms and rings that will dazzle all eyes so they can't see your freckles, and lockets that will snap in and hold the hearts of your lovers."

Such was the burden of my song, and by the time I had gotten half through it, and given my audience a peep in my box, all the females of the family, Mam, Sis and Pussy, were busy, not at their proper and usual work, but in overhauling my goods and dickering for such of them as took their fancy; and once started at buying they would see this, that and the other article, the want of which they never before felt need of, but now were certain they could never be happy without, and the, to me, sweet buy and buy would be kept up so long as they had a coin to spend.

How often in those days I realized the truth of the old adage that "a fool and his money are soon parted;" but as I was not the fool, and the money was coming to, not parting from me, I did nothing necessary to remind my customers of the ancient proverb.

Spectacles were probably the most profitable articles in my stock; for these there was a large and steady demand, and the manner in which I worked off dozen after dozen, I here tell, not to instruct others in deceitful practices, but as a warning to the short-sighted and unsophisticated of impaired vision, who require the information to protect them, from further imposition.

The profit on one pair of "specs" would pay expenses for a whole day, and I always worked hard to realize that amount from said source. The more elderly men and women of that section, almost without exception, used glasses; they were, most of them, never willing to admit that their eye sight was failing, or their old pair not of sufficient magnifying power; it was "the glasses were scratched," or "they never had suited," or some other fault.

Most certainly did I join in with their abuse of the pair then in possession; another pair more powerful would be produced from my box, properly lectured over, and "sold again, and got the money," would be my joyful but inaudible song.

Occasionally I would find an individual who asserted that he or she was perfectly satisfied and admirably suited with the old eye aids, and needed or would have no new ones. It was then no part of my plan to disparage the ancient stand-bys; I asked to see them, handled them with an air of veneration, passed my finger over the surface of the glasses (having first inserted the finger in my ear and gathered upon it a light coating of waxy secretion), and so rendered them somewhat blurred or dim. I would then hand them back without a word against them; but soon I asked the wearers, as a favor and experiment, to try just for a

A BIG "SPEC" IN SPECS. moment, and simply as an illustration of the inventive and improving genius of the age; a glimpse through a pair of my "new patent, back-action, triple-lens, corner-concave, gas magnifying, microscopic multiplying, diamond polished, Cape of Good Hope pebble, Amsterdam cut, eye invigorating, intensifying and regenerating spectacles." And it was ten chances to one that I had the cash for the new pair, and at an extra price too, in my pocket within five minutes.

Then I used to have three or four pairs stowed away down at the bottom of my box; these I was "keeping for" some local celebrity of high repute, and I never appeared anxious to sell them, in fact I pretended to be rather shy of, and sly about exhibiting or having them handled; but as a "special favor" to the party then undergoing manipulation, I would just show them "a pair of particularly fine glasses, extra gem-lens I was taking to" the Judge or Minister or some other influential individual.

Of course these "special specs" were of high perfection and price, so I stated, and it was a rarely self-sacrificing or strong minded person who, having once tried them on, did not discover their wonderful superiority over all others, did not insist upon retaining them, and paying therefor a price three times as great as that for which I could have obtained the exact duplicates by taking any of those I had with me.

I will not, even in this truthful chronicle, "give away" what I paid wholesale price for this most valuable portion of my trading outfit; but the profit on each pair, even if they brought but two dollars, (and they generally sold for much more), was large, very large.

Great P. T. Barnum is credited with the saying, that "people of this country love to be humbugged," and I am prepared to endorse the opinion of that wise and successful showman.

The pair of spectacles for which I received five dollars, the man who bought them would have refused to look at had I offered them at two dollars or less, saying and thinking that at such a low figure they must necessarily be good for nothing. When I sold brass jewelry at fifty cents a set, I had hard work to get rid of it; but when I displayed the very same goods as extra fine, latest style, quadruple gilt, and added two dollars to their price, they "went off like hot cakes," and every girl who had earned, could earn, or borrow, or coax from father, mother, brother, husband or lover the sum required, was hunting around for me to take her money and furnish her with the trash.

STUCK.

Such is life, and the deceitfulness of mankind; especially peddlers.

In compliance with my rule "to be all things to all men," my political sentiments and religious convictions were invariably stretched or contracted, rounded off or smoothed out, to coincide exactly with those of the party with whom I was trading or stopping for the time.

More than once I was placed in most embarrassing predicaments in attempting to accommodate myself to circumstances, where I fit about as compactly as a "round man in a square hole."

I had a tight squeeze with a Methodist minister, at whose house I stopped over night, I had, of course, given him to understand that I was a devoted follower of John Wesley, and that evening he asked me to "lead in prayer." I attempted to comply with his request, but in very shame my tongue refused utterance and my mind to frame ideas. I was "stuck," and finally told him that I only could, and always did offer up my prayers in my native Danish—an explanation he seemed to consider decidedly thin. He advised me to cultivate fluency in English for devotional purposes as carefully and assiduously as I did for transactions in peddling.

Another time I sadly missed hitting it when, on arriving at a ferry I found the "ferryman" was four buxom females. I reached the house on the river bank just as they were departing, gorgeously arrayed for some quilting or country dance, and congratulated myself upon arriving before they left. I entered into conversation with them, thinking that I might make sales and defray ferry and other expenses, and in course of general chatter I mentioned that I had served in the Union army during the war.

That settled it, but not in the least to my satisfaction. The four female ferryites flamed furiously forth at once; "they were Pike county, Missouri women, they were!" and rebels of the deepest dye, and I was a "bloody Hessian, who had sold myself to the Yankees and aided in killing their fathers, husbands, brothers and lovers." If I waited for them to take me across the river I would most likely die of old age on that bank. They grew warmer and warmer until words failed to express their opinion of me, and action took the place of speech. They opened fire

FOUR FURIOUS FEMALES.

upon me with mud and rocks, and I only escaped bodily injury by putting my pack on my head and wading to the opposite shore.

But such unpleasant encounters were very few in my Oregon experiences; travelling through that country is a succession of joys for every sense; the soil is most fertile, bringing forth plenteous crops with the least expenditure of labor, refreshing rains are frequent, the climate is delightful and invigorating, the rivers teem with fish of choice varieties, and the hills abound in game.

The indian inhabitants of that Territory are all well-behaved and on reservations, controlled and fed by the government. I mingled much among the red men, for whom my glistening trinkets possessed many attractions, and in return for jewelry, knives, beads and knick-knacks generally, I obtained many of the valuable furs which they know so well how to prepare, on which I realized a profit over which I certainly never complained.

CHAPTER XXI.
DOWN TO THE BOTTOM AGAIN.

I made three trips through Oregon, constantly increasing my capital and popularity.

Returning to Portland to replenish my travelling box from stock in my store trunk, I found that the landlord of the hotel where I always stopped, and with whom I had left the trunk, had attached my property as security for a debt of $200, due him from my quasi friend Dr. Slagimdote.

In answer to my indignant demand to know what I, my trunk or goods had to do with the debts of anybody but myself, he replied that I had endorsed or become responsible for the account of that individual. This I emphatically denied, though I acknowledged that, when the landlord once asked me, "How about the Doctor?" I had carelessly replied, "Oh, he's all right," or words to that effect.

This admission, in the legal mind of the veritable Dogberry of a Squire, before whom the case was brought for trial, was considered to hold good as though I had given

THE DOCTOR'S HOTEL BILL.

written security for the honesty of Dr. S., and I was accordingly "let in" for the amount.

I had engaged a "shyster" lawyer to conduct the defence on part of myself and the doctor, but his services did more harm than good, and I was forced to hand him over as a fee, not only all that remained of my stock of goods, but also two silver watches whereof I had become possessed.

I learned later that a desire for revenge had caused the institution of this suit, the doctor being the man against whom hatred was directed, for

not only had he contracted debts wherever he could find anyone to trust him, but he had also entered and indulged in a career of debauchery which knew no limit, including among his victims the young wife of the hotel keeper;

SOME OF THE DR'S WORK.

the poor woman soon after becoming insane and dying by her own hand.

It was to retaliate in some measure upon this grand rascal that the prosecution was entered, but I was made the sufferer. All these hidden motives did not become known to me until much later, and just then, won by his seeming sorrow and deceived by his lying explanations, feeling likewise utterly broken down and adrift in the world, with all my bright prospects and hopes completely blasted by undeserved punishment, I considered him a brother in misfortune and I stuck to him.

By selling some of my personal property I managed to get money enough to take the two of us to San Francisco, having hard work to smuggle the doctor on board the steamer without the knowledge of those who were gunning for him, but I contrived to give them the slip, and we reached a new port safely.

The medical Jonah who had caused my financial and commercial shipwreck, found in 'Frisco a partner worthy of him, one of the same craft and craftiness, and together they opened an office and sought for practice, while I served them in every capacity in order to earn enough to keep from starving.

In return for the thirty or forty cents a day which they gave me, while

I frequented the hotels, depots, landings and places of resort in search of steady work, whenever I spied an honest miner, emigrant or any one else who gave the least evidences of suffering from shakes of ague, snakes of whisky, or any other sickness, and with whom I had or made acquaintance, I condoled with and advised them as a friend the best course to pursue, and if possible I would "run him in" as a patient to the medical partners, who were really excellent physicians.

If my picked up patient yielded any money, I was allowed a dollar or fraction thereof for my share, as a commission.

THE DOCTOR'S DRUMMER.

That this was not a very high-toned course I am fully aware, and I was very much ashamed to be thus engaged, but necessity knows no law and acknowledges no moral obligations. I might have been at worse work, it is true, and I ought to have been at much better. •

I became more and more disgusted with my miserable and degrading manner of life, of gleaning or scraping only starvation gains as a barker for the poison mill of Slagimdote & Co. I slowly but surely gained an insight into this man's true character and whole course of proceedings.

My eyes were opened at last, and I could see what an easily blinded fool I had been, how he had at the first, when I possessed money, merely looked upon me as a poor dupe who could and would act as his banker, and now finding me still a willing victim of his wiles, he allowed me to serve as his lackey.

He owed me not only the amount of the hotel bill I had been forced to pay, but for money borrowed on many occasions, cash spent for his travelling and living expenses and pleasures; fact is, he drained me by every means in his power without conscience or mercy. It was time for me to "kick."

Fully realizing that I could never expect to recover a cent from him, I resolved to make a desperate effort to regain at least a portion of my loss by appealing to his father, and as a preliminary step to such action I dissolved my connection with the medical institute of Slagimdote & Co.

I next hunted up the paternal Slagimdote, likewise an M. D., and with all the eloquence that could be excited by outraged feelings, poverty and despair, I poured out to him the story of my wrongs, detailed the acts of which his son had been guilty, avowed my innocence of any participation in his ill deeds, my losses through him, and my pressing necessities,

The consolation, advice, aid and comfort I received from this ancient sinner, of whom one might reverse the old adage and say "like son, so father," was contained in the abrupt.

"Served you right! just right! Any one but a born fool would have seen at a glance that my son was a worthless rascal and common swindler. I won't pay a cent for him or give a cent to him, I've done it before but I'll never do it again, I'm done with him forever!"

Under pretence of offering me what compensation he could for the misery brought upon me by his son, but really, I believe, because he saw that he could get more work out of me for less money than any one else he could hire, the elder S. proposed that I come to live with him as a man of all work, at thirty dollars per month wages.

Badly in want of some place to call a home, I engaged with the old man and at once entered upon his service. "Man of all work" truly was I, cook, errand boy, house servant, stable man, boot black, pill maker, potion mixer, milkmaid, chicken tender, companion and slave.

The senior M. D. was as detestable in his miserly meanness as was his son in his dishonesty and debauchery. The milk from the cows he kept, he sold yet begrudged them food to enable them to produce the fluid, and continually abused me for supplying them with fodder sufficient for their subsistence. He would have counted every grain thrown out to the fowls, and yet he expected the poor things to lay eggs.

SENIOR SLAGIMDOTE'S STARVATION STOCK.

The cows gave but little milk, and I used to supply our customers with the unadulterated article, the small share the old man reserved for his own use, I watered well when we ran short. I had my meals at the same table with him, and every morning he indulged himself with two eggs, while I was obliged to ration on bread and barley coffee, which latter he considered far more healthy (and cheaper) than the genuine bean.

I didn't propose to starve though, and as he swallowed his two eggs and pump milk at the table, I absorbed what "hen fruit" and "cow juice" I considered necessary for my health and strength, at the place of their production, and thus managed to get even on the grub question.

I stuck it out with this old screw for some time, but finally we became involved in a wordy quarrel over some of his petty meanness and I cut loose from him. I must do him the justice to say that he paid me every penny promised or due me, and I never heard of him refusing to meet any contract he made. But he was close, very close.

GETTING EVEN.

I hunted up my old kink-haired, dark complexioned, soap boiling friend and former boss, and with him found work and "white man" treatment which kept me busy at the fat tub until May, 1867, when I obtained employment as laborer at the Mare Island Navy Yard, and continued there for some time.

Next I shifted my body and talents to Benecia, and exercised both as hostler in a livery stable attached to a hotel. Among those four-legged Christians, the horses, I lived in a fair state of content, earning thirty dollars a month, until the periodical fit of restlessness again seized upon me, and being unable to resist the pressure, I announced my intention of moving on, or off, an idea that the land-lady of the hotel so violently opposed that I had hard work to gain possession of my wages and make my escape.

To Annsdale I moved, and there obtained a job in a cement mill. At this I worked steadily until the mill shut down, and then I was forced to resume my travels. I drifted back to San Francisco, and for two weeks remained in idleness, with the exception of two days, when I labored on the water works near Fort Point.

This kind of business, or want of it, would never do; it was absolutely necessary for me to hustle around and earn my grub. I hustled.

CHAPTER XXII.

PICKING UP A LITTLE.

It was now three years since I had first arrived in California; I had struggled hard to deserve good and fight against ill fortune, toiled faithfully for success, but found it not.

I was worse off, in everything but experience, than when I had entered the State. The Coast line had not been a Golden Shore to me, the tides in my affairs were many and all led on to fortune of the worst sort. The necessity of "hustling" was forced upon me by a stomach clamorous for food and a body that sadly required re-clothing.

Certain that I could be no worse, and any change being for the better, calling up what of hope and courage I could, with just about a dollar to live on, I started for Sacramento, intending to tramp; but just then came a season of cut rates, opposition, slaughtering tactics and fighting between rival railroads, and I was able to buy a ticket for my destination for twenty-five cents. "Its an ill wind that blows nobody good," can truly be said of the occasional blizzards that howl between rival transporting companies; though the general public have to make up all losses in the long run.

No more demand existing for my services in Sacramento, I "hoofed it" to Cisco, ninety miles further inland, the termination at that time of the Central Pacific Railroad, where much work was doing in the rock cutting necessary for the extension of that line.

At this point I secured work as a laborer, and found myself a stranger and novice among men who were professional experts at this kind of toil, and also highly accomplished masters of the whole art of shirking duty and loafing during work hours, when the boss was not about ; they had reduced the matter to a perfect science.

I always believed in doing what I had contracted to perform, so plunged ahead, always anxious to do my level best, and keeping up the steady blows of my heavy sledge upon the drill which my mate held and

directed, whether the overseer was within sight or not, much to the disgust of my "pard," who with the rest of the gang set me down as a big fool in general, and he considered me a confounded nuisance to himself in particular.

I was by no means surprised at the character I gained in the estimation of my companions, for all my unnecessary toil, as they considered it, but I was certainly highly astonished at the result of this giving of a fair day's labor for a fair day's wages.

The boss of our section, who knew his business well, soon noticed that work did not proceed during his absence, at the same rate and rapid-

ROCK CUTTING.

ity which marked its growth while he was on the ground, and easily suspecting, or fully aware of the cause of such uneven results, he stationed himself at a distance, where, through

the aid of a powerful field glass, he could easily watch operations without the gang being aware that his eye was upon them.

Thus he made himself master of the whole situation, and as I continually busied myself about something, even when my "butty" would drop his drill and refuse to hold it in loafing time ; I was focused in the boss' eye as a steady, honest worker, while others were identified as habitual shirkers. I don't say that I never, not even for a moment, took a small, short loaf, but I did

A SLY OLD BOSS.

not overdo the matter and was lucky enough to escape detection.

The first intimation I had of the favor gained by my industry, was when the boss walked up to and accosted me.

"Here, young fellow, you throw down that hammer, and you need never take it up again on this work unless it is to show some one else how to use it."

I obeyed his order promptly. He led me over to a dirt cutting and installed me as boss over thirty-five Chinamen, and I felt as proud as though I had received a commission of Major General. It was an easy job I had now, and I bossed my yellow boys in dignified comfort, having no

AN EASY JOB.

THE BIG BAGGAGE BOUNCER.

SNOW SHOEING.

trouble in getting good work out of them, and giving every satisfaction to my superiors. But I desired, as winter was coming on, to find a place where I would not be exposed so much to the severely inclement weather of that section, and after I had been overseer in the dirt cut for some weeks, I made application for work such as I proposed to do, and was transferred to the depot of the company at Cisco, where my bulk of body and strength of back stood me in good part as the big baggage bouncer and wrestler with the heavy freight generally.

Winter set in very early that season, and was unusually frigid, the snow drifts in many places being twenty feet deep; travel was almost entirely suspended and I had little and light work to do in the freight department of that station.

But my services were soon brought into requisition by my assignment as "line man" on the wire extending over the Sierra Nevada Mountains, my duties in this connection consisting of general supervision of the iron thread, hunting out breaks, dragging detached wires from the snow and re-uniting them, carrying messages and odd jobs of every decription. The snow rendered it necessary to wear snow shoes, which while differing in style from those used in Canada were equally efficacious, and I soon learned to "handle my feet;" thus equipped, with ease, safety and celerity, and many a mile I thus traversed upon the snowy surface over vast solitudes.

This work was very laborious, always attended with more or less danger, yet it had in it an element of excitement that just suited me, and I enjoyed the life immensely. Often my escapes were little short of miraculous, and many times I came near to losing my life in the snow. On one occasion I wandered from my path at night and was compelled to employ every moment of time in active movement of as many of my muscles at the same moment as possible, dancing, running, jumping, etc., continually, for I knew that to remain quiet for even the shortest period, meant frozen to death, and these gymnastics I kept up until morning light enabled me to ascertain my whereabouts and exert my efforts in reaching the station.

With all this to combat, I would have been perfectly content with my life had not the demon of desire for change again entered my brains and made me take action which resulted in another change of situation.

CHAPTER XXIII.
ON THE FRONTIER.

I had long entertained a great desire to see something of life on the frontier, but did not wish to seek experiences in the garb or station of a private soldier as one of the regular army.

I heard that a surveying party was soon to start out, and I bestirred myself to obtain a position therein, and early in the year 1868, I was gratified by an appointment as "stake marker," with orders to report in person at Hunter's Station, now called Reno; from which our detail set out to meet and aid another party in laying out preliminary lines for what is now the Grand Central Pacific Railroad. Our chief engineer was named Cadwallader.

Beginning at the Sink of the Humbolt River, we followed closely up the line of that stream, including in our survey the work in Twelve Mile Canyon, beyond Carlin, around the cliffs of the Pallisades, on through Five Mile Canyon, as wildly beautiful, grand and picturesque country as is to be found upon the face of the earth.

Our section was in the advance, the engineer in charge of it was Mr. Bates, a good, easy going gentleman, a thorough master of his profession, and very fond of peace at any cost; by him, in addition to my stake driving, I was placed in the responsible position of mule driver, and in this second attempt to acquire the mysteries ot that science, I acquired some proficiency therein.

The party muster in all, twelve men, two

ON THE HUMBOLT.   of these being only teamsters.   The life was all that was enjoyable, being healthy, exciting, varied and most romantic, with just sufficient of danger and risk to cause us to be on the keen lookout for human and other enemies.

We were frequently brought in contact with the Indians of that locality, and as we were moving far in advance of civilization and its refinements, we interviewed the aborigines in all their native simplicity of dress, or rather undress, manners and customs.

Ample opportunities were afforded us to learn and study the cunning, cruelty, ignorance, brutality, superstitions and general habits—all very filthy ones—of these "noble sons of the forest;" and all our observations tended to impress upon our minds the strong belief that they would not, under any circumstances, be particularly pleasant additions to a small evening tea party, or the sacred limits of a home circle.

The "Noble Indian" is a good deal of a humbug, so far as I can judge, and most likely never existed except in the vivid and generous imagination of those who wrote of but

never knew them, the "Dirty Injun" is a deplorable, disgusting, unnecessary, existing fact.

Our party was sufficiently large, and all so well provided with weapons of offense and defence, that the foolishness of getting up any fight with us was apparent, even to the savage intellects with which we were constantly exchanging compliments, so no hostile demonstrations were made against us, decidedly friendly overtures taking the place of bloody outrages, and we took advantage of such disposition for peace and good will, to vary our bill of fare by trading flour, bread, sugar and coffee with the natives for game and fish.

UNNECESSARY FACTS.

The country through which we were carrying our survey was by no means level and adapted to easy or graceful locomotion, the contrary was the bone-breaking actuality. The whole of mother earth's surface out there seemed to be broken up in lots of every imaginable size, and care taken to set each of these up edgeways, so our daily pilgrimage and the prosecution of our work necessitated and consisted mostly in a series of climbings up and over rocks, and scramblings down into chasms, and when not thus engaged we were fighting, tearing and cutting our way through thick underbrush, wading bogs and swamps, or fording rivers of all widths and depths.

A diversion we enjoyed at all times, the material being over plentiful, was destruction of the principal product of that territory over which we were tramping, rattlesnakes ; rattlesnakes, big, little and medium, there was no end, the earth, stones, bushes, everything, seemed to breed rattlesnakes.

How many of these horrible reptiles I killed I do not know. I kept count in my mind and tally by fastening the rattles on my hat (a fashion we all much affected) until I was tired of remembering and adding to the numbers, and my hat had no space left for further rattle ornamentation, as the old song says, "all around my hat I wore 'em."

I escaped all danger from the fangs of the

"ALL 'ROUND MY 'AT I WEARS 'EM."

snakes, but I had one encounter with the Indians which came near being "deadly pizen" to me.

CHAPTER XXIV.
FRONTIER FIGHTS AND FANCIES.

My little difficulty with the Indians happened thus :
We had pitched a new camp about six miles up the Humbolt, to which we were about to remove, but as yet had not occupied it, and I was sent to guard what property had been taken there.' I was all alone, but felt little fear of any attack being made upon me, and if one was commenced I was well provided with means of resistance, having at hand six carbines, a Henry repeating rifle, two revolvers, and plenty of ammunition.

I was good for a moderate sized tribe as long as I was able to take aim and draw trigger.

About dusk of evening I was surprised to see four strange, stalwart, well armed Indian bucks come stalking into camp. They looked around, examining all arrangements, then perceiving and understanding that I had no companions ; their manner grew each minute more insolent and threatening, evidently depending upon their superiority in numbers to force or awe me into submission.

They did not ask for, but curtly demanded that I should give them food, and I, as was the custom of our party, furnished them with all the provender I thought they required at that time. They then insisted that I should supply them with provisions to carry away, likewise with powder for their rifles.

In reply to their modest requests, I told them very decidedly that they would not get either grub or powder from me, but that they should git up and git out of that camp, or they would find powder and ball more plenty than they wished.

My orders to them were well understood, and I uttered them with a very bold and confident air, assuming a manner that implied ability to enforce obedience. So my uninvited guests turned about and moved sullenly away, going into camp about half a mile distant.

I kept a very close watch upon them, as I had learned and understood sufficient of Indian character and methods to feel certain that these fellows would, before next morning, pay my quarters another visit to get, or try to get, by stealth or violence, what they could not obtain by begging.

I knew that if I allowed myself to sleep that night, the probabilities were of the strongest kind against my ever waking up in this world. My religious convictions did not assure me that a transfer to the world of
"GIT UP AND GIT, INJUN." spirits would in the least add to my comfort ; anyhow, this world was good enough for me to sleep and wake in for some time to come, and I concluded that there should be no dead Danish Hans in that locality if I could help it, and I made my arrangements accordingly.

Just so soon as it became sufficiently dark to prevent the keen eyes of these dusky thieves from detecting my movements, I carried away from the spot where they had seen them, all the supplies which had been placed under my care, and secreted the lots as best I could in different places.

With the fighting goods, the weapons, I stationed myself about fifty feet from my former location, and covering my position as well as I could, I went "into battery," laid my plans carefully and my tools handy, made desperate resolves to keep awake all that night, and to reorganize my manner of living in the future, said about a dozen prayers of a dozen-deacon-power each and waited.

Waiting under such circumstances, straining eyes to peer through the darkness, and ear drums to catch the faintest sound, is about as hard work on body and brain as a man wants to tackle. It is wearing on the nerves to wait in the dark alone for danger that will certainly come, but from what direction you know not; its harder work than fighting, and I had more than enough of it that night.

With every sense at its utmost tension I watched and waited, I know not how long, but it seemed hours, days, months. At last I heard sounds of disappointment and rage proceeding from the spot I had left. I knew the sources from which those grunts came, and I opened fire all along the line.

I saluted every point of the compass, and all intermediate radiations with shots from the sixteen shooter Henry rifle, sent whistling in all directions the bullets from the six carbines, peppered into the surrounding darkness the balls from both chambers of my revolvers, and then I fell back in good order to refit, load up my ordnance stores and get ready for another shot salute to all creation, if necessary.

Then I began to feel good, much of my nervousness I had blown away with the powder I exploded; I was satisfied that the "marauding foe," as a romance writer would term them, were fully aware that there was somebody in that immediate vicinity, who was in possession of a varied assortment of firearms, and reckless in his consumption of ammunition.

Soon I felt better than good, I had no more thought of saying my prayers, either in petitions for aid or songs of thanksgiving. I heard no further sounds of the enemy, but I kept up keen watch, thinking neither of sleep or venturing forth until the broadest of broad day light enabled me to get full range of all the surrounding country.

When I returned to the camping ground I found evidences of the prowlers' visit, but no killed or wounded, and I had no further visits from the redskins, which suited my book exactly; all I wanted was to be let alone. But I am well satisfied that if I had gone to sleep or remained on that spot that night, there would have been "cold meat" there the next morning, and I would not have been able to eat it.

With the exception of such little interruptions as that just mentioned, I pursued the even tenor of my way with the surveying party, and gradually began, by observation and practice, to imbibe a certain knowledge of the art, or to have such instinct awakened within me, and I also acquired a habit of viewing the landscape over which we were passing with the eye of an expert, or one who thought himself to be such.

I was continually making mental record of choice locations for town sites, cities, central depots, manufacturing villages, farms, etc., and this was a source of constant pleasure to me as we kept on our route and work up the Humbolt River.

CHAPTER XXV.
DREAMS AND REALITIES.

The month of July, 1868, brought our party as far as South Forks, twelve miles below the site of the present town of Elko.

Here my eyes were dazzled by sight of a plateau of land, which appeared to me to be a veritable corner lot from the Garden of Eden, sliced off and dumped into this spot for my special pleasure and benefit.

With that promptness of action which becomes, or should do so, second nature to every man who roughs it on the frontier, I at once determined that on this delectable land I would pitch my tent and make me a habitation and a home.

It was not many minutes then, before I had, in full compliance with border laws, regulations and customs, driven my stakes and posted notice that I had and thereby did, pre-empted, taken up and claimed "all that section or parcel of land running 2,640 feet from stake South, to 2,640 feet, stake West ; same width to stake beginning," all of which made a quarter section of land, AND IT WAS MINE OWN.

Back of my claim there was nothing but range on range of hills, but my quarter section was a garden spot, every inch rich with deep, black, fertile soil; all being the very best of grazing land.

Let my most excitable reader imagine his wildest dreams of prosperity about to be realized, and he will hardly equal the extravagant speculations in which I indulged over that land. I could fill page after page with exact descriptions of the architectural peculiarities of the many air castles I erected on that earth, the amount of the ever growing wealth that was to come rolling in upon me, the droves of cattle and flocks and herds that were soon to roam, unnumbered and innumerable upon those hills, that formed so noble a background to my new-found paradise, all these thoughts filled my waking moments and my hours of slumber.

But the stern demands of every-day life and the unsentimental duties connected with stake and mule driving would not permit of my remaining in the clouds and visionary bliss, I had to "step down and out."

I was obliged to buckle to my work and I did so with a feeling of satisfaction that every day of surveying labor, the cash therefor and regular rations for stomach, were much more substantial, and comfortably filling, than misty loiterings in dream-land and a diet of wind puddings. So I continued with the party all summer, a rather protracted stretch of easy sailing for me.

But the inevitable row and change were coming.

When we had reached the neighborhood of Promontory the cook of our party made up his mind to depart. He so did. Mr. Bates had discovered that the culinary art was comprised among my many accomplishments and he urged me to take upon myself the honors of the pots and pans, and to oblige him I consented.

The inevitable war and curses that are accompaniments of the broils, stews and messes of every camp and ship cook's life, soon commenced and involved me in broils, stews and messes, that finally boiled over and landed me out of the cook-tent, out of the camp, and out of a job.

There was one of the party who looked with the green eyes of jaundiced jealousy upon what he considered my undeserved promotion to the Kitchen Cabinet, for the reason that he desired the position himself.

From the day of my inauguration he commenced and persisted in finding fault with every dish of food, and to his dissatisfaction he gave free and vigorous expression in language which was not only calculated to wound my pride as an artist, but was highly offensive to me individually.

He asserted that I knew nothing, absolutely nothing, about cooking, that I wasted and rendered uneatable the provisions. With profanity and untruthfulness he stigmatized me as a "Beastly, dirty Dutchman!"

I had lost in a great measure, that indifference to verbal and physical abuse, which in my former life seemed to be born of patience, fear or sloth; and this miscalling of my nationality and averment of my uncleanliness, roused the Danish fighting blood within me and I "went for" the libelous liar all I knew how.

The fight was a good, clear, knock down and drag out, and two friends of my opponent, seeing that he had undertaken a larger contract than

PLUCK, LUCK AND PICK-HANDLE.

he could fill in "getting away with me," generously mixed in, but by gathering up and exercising all my strength, and a pick handle, completely routed the combined forces of the enemy and drove them off the field.

They retired in not very good order or humor, held a council of war, and then renewed the battle, with artillery, in the shape of their pistols, well in front.

My shooting irons were not within reach. I retreated for change of base; I don't say that I ran away, but I walked very fast in the opposite direction from the wrathful men who were pointing pistols, loaded and cocked, with awfully careless fingers on triggers; in direction of my brain pan.

I did not return to camp for some hours after retiring from the combat, and when I got back and hunted up my weapons, I found that these fellows had, in a spirit of wanton vindictiveness, taken my much prized Henry rifle, extracted from it all the cartridges, and destroyed my entire stock of ammunition. I had cooled down considerably before I discovered this mean trick, and the outrage was a fresh *casus belli*. The battle commenced anew and raged furiously; this time, however, hostilities were confined to language, and in it the chief of our party, Mr. Bates, took a share.

Our leader soon discovered that peace was neither to be patched up or preserved between my antagonists and myself and he was forced to allow policy to get the better of justice, as the question was whether he should lose one man or three, at a time when he could illy spare any from his gang. There was no other solution to the matter, no other course open to him,

1 must go; to send the three friends off at that stage of the work would have crippled him too severely to be thought of and been a violation of his duty to the company.

He told me, regretfully, that I was to consider myself "bounced;" paid me in full for six months' service, at forty dollars a month; gave me one hundred rounds of cartridges for my Henry rifle (all he could spare from his own stock of ammunition); his blessings and good wishes; and I went.

Loaded like a pack-mule, with my trusty weapon, blankets, clothing, cooking utensils, six days' rations, a sense of ill treatment and the curses and jeers of my enemies, I turned my back upon the surveying party and business, and struck out on the trail to retrace my steps to South Fork and my "Land of Goshen."

OFF FOR THE LAND OF GOSHEN.

How I did hoof it over ground to my beauty spot!

I was burning with impatience to satisfy myself by eye evidence that it was really there, and that the whole matter was not a creation of imagination, and highly delighted was I when I once more stood upon "my land."

At once I proceeded to build a hut that would serve me as winter quarters, and then I settled down to try the life of a hermit; and it proved the most "trying" life of all the many varieties in which I had ever been thrown or voluntarily placed myself.

AS A HERMIT.

As a hermit, I was not a happy success.

CHAPTER XXVI.
TRYING A TURN AS TEAMSTER.

My life, after I entered into possession of, and residence upon my property was about as lively as it would have been in a quaker burying-ground on a dark night in December.

The beasts of the field and birds of the air were the only companions I had for most of the time; the few human beings that crossed my path were the teamsters who passed by, and from these I obtained a little news and whatsoever of provisions I required.

The Robinson Crusoe trade of "living all alone by yourself" and being "monarch of all I survey" was very comfortable, lazy, and luxurious existence for a time, nothing to do but to cook, sleep and eat.

But I had always been an animal of social, though quiet, disposition, and the charms of solitude began to pall upon me as the monotony of my life each day increased. I tried to reconcile myself to steady continuance in the hermit line; but, like Paddy who "got blue mouldy for want uv a batin'," I soon began to long for the changeful life and stirring scenes to which I had been accustomed, and I cast about for ways and methods to satisfy my desire.

Prudence and frugality of expenditure and living in the past months of steady employment had once more placed me in possession of, to me considerable, available capital, and I decided to invest a portion of my funds in an outfit for active business.

The transportation trade seemed to be doing thrivingly in that section and with a view to entering into it I purchased two horses and a wagon, the outlay for these walking into my "pile" to the tune of $350.

But I was so fortunate as to find quick and steady demand for my services and was kept busy in carrying freight from the completed end of the railroad to the advanced Camp of Construction; supplies needed by the gangs who were preparing the road bed for the track layers.

Hauling heavy loads over those unbroken, new roads, was no easy work on man, horses or wagon; my vexations and mishaps, delays, tilt ups, break downs, and turn overs, were very numerous.

One day I was freighted with three heavy boxes, weighing over six hundred pounds each, a very stiff load for that country; and was crossing, or trying to cross, over a flat, when the wheels became mired up to the hubs and it was impossible for the horses to budge the wagon.

I coaxed, and pulled, and whipped, and jerked, and exhorted the animals to the extent of my ability, strength and language, but without effect.

A STICK IN THE MUD.

The team could not do the work, and I was resting my tired bones and tongue when along came a six-mule team.

To the captain of this land schooner I made known my unfortunate fix; in fact he spied and enjoyed it, and to him I applied for assistance.

But prayers, abuse, or promises to pay would not move the hard heart of this prairie pirate to pity and lending of a helping hand or mule. With unnecessary and profuse profanity, he informed me that such small, two-horse concerns as mine had no business to try hauling on that road, taking business from the regularly equipped and thoroughly efficient six-mule team monopolies.

He said I was now in my proper place, my team also; being but a "stick in the mud" of a freighter, and he considered it due to personal pride, professional honor, and the interests of his employers, to leave me where he found me and where I belonged. He left me.

In gay disdain, and gleeful contempt he departed, sarcastically hurling at me the advice and philosophy of his class, as expressed in the obscene doggerel, "If you want to get rich, etc., you must paddle your own canoe."

This addition of insult to injury aroused my angry passions to a most fervent heat, and for a few moments I was tempted to have recourse to "border law," to follow the inhuman brute up and with a pistol shot let a little sunlight into his dark interior. But a few moments of reflection turned the current of my thoughts and saved me from a murderous act.

Arousing myself once more to exertion, I unharnessed and picketed my horses away from the mire, I fed the poor, tired animals, and then, taking a rope, chain and axe, I walked three miles to the mountains and growing timber and cut two long poles with which, by using them as levers, I hoped to raise my wagon from its miry bed.

These poles I lugged and dragged back, paddling my own canoe, over the long, rough road, and with this aid I managed to roll the heavy boxes off into the grass, and then to pry out the wagon next by the hardest of straining, I replaced my bulky load and proceeded on my way to Elko in a much happier frame of mind and far better satisfied with myself and the world.

As I tramped along and turned my latest experience over, I argued myself into belief that the rough, but not ready, uncharitable, and disobliging six mule team aristocrat had really conferred upon me,

PADDLING MY OWN CANOE.

without intending so to do, valuable advice and instruction, when he left me to get out a bad case of stuck-in-the-mud, solely by my own wits and exertions.

The parting injunction to "paddle your own canoe," I have ever since remembered ; acting upon it also as a sound working principle, and in most matters of business, where I have relied and acted upon this philosophy, I have been successful.

I had an occasional glimpse of original or aboriginal life during my first stay at South Fork Farm, through occasional visitors, who, though their comings were "few and far between," had nothing angelic about them. They were Indians.

The subject-matter of their first call was to inform me that "this Injun water, Injun land, Injun game," in fact, it was, according to them, "all Injun," and "no white man need apply."

The spokesman of the party grunted out the invitation to leave in the English he had picked up from the miners with an air of menace that told more plainly than his words, that if I didn't go willingly I'd be made to go by force.

I had, however, lived too long in the woods to be scared by owls or Injuns either, and had also learned that Brag was often a good helping dog to Holdfast, and so I set the first named to barking.

Mr. Redman was notified that I was "Big Chief," with many soldiers at my call from Camp Halleck, which was about forty miles over the hills, and that I intended to stay. My Henry repeater was something new in the way of fire-arms to them ; I told them it was a devil-gun, and putting my hat at about fifty paces distant, I fired eleven balls through the crown more quickly than they could count the shots, and then intimated that I could keep on popping away all day without re-loading.

 The exhibition of this wonderful gun, my cheek and oratory, changed their style somewhat, and when I gave them some of my provisions they became rather friendly.

Some of them had seen me with the surveying party, and heard me called "Dutchman," and by that name I was known to them.

At each visit we came to a better understanding, and accident enabled me to acquire very considerable influence over them.

Two of the party came to me one day and told me that a party of cavalry men had taken their guns. I had pen, ink, and paper, and I at once wrote to the commanding officer, acquainting him with the facts, telling him that these were good Indians, and asking him to see justice done.

With "the paper that talks" the bucks made their way to the party that had disarmed them and had their property restored, in addition receiving two old guns, two ancient blankets, and a lot of maggotty bacon. They came back to me delighted ; I crowed immensely, asserting that I was the big chief who had done it all, and they fully believed me. Game of all kinds was shared with me whenever they had it, and I was not mean about giving what I could spare out of my own supplies.

Another matter that added to my importance was the breaking out among them of the small-pox. They were entirely ignorant of any remedy; I had previously done a little doctoring among them, and, as a wise, big chief, they came to me for advice and assistance.

I went to Elko, and obtained information and medicine from the doctor there, then went back to their camp, my clothing deluged with carbolic acid, smelling "loud" enough to disinfect the entire territory, and by the use of the remedies I brought, and common-sense care I ordered, nearly all recovered, and I had the highest of Indian honors as BIG MEDICINE MAN.

From that time there was nothing they would not do for me. I could leave my cabin unlocked, my provisions on the table, everything dear to the Indian heart within reach of them, and they neither touched or tasted without invitation or permission.

Any one acquainted with the Indian character will understand how strong was my influence with them when I say that on one occasion I accused the young son of a chief of stealing my lariat rope, and gave him a thrashing. This would have been a killing matter for most men, but the old chief and others hunted around for means to convince me that I was in the wrong, and they did so.

They came to me and bade me follow the trail left by the lariat, and plainly showed me how it had been dragged off by a prowling coyote, and led me to its den, where I found the rope. Then I felt like kicking myself, and with apologies and liberal expenditure of my store, I made the matter right so far as they were concerned, but I always felt "cheap" over it.

I did considerable trapping with these new friends, and they gave me the beaver and other skins, satisfying themselves with. the meat, which they greatly relished, though it was too oily for my taste, and I only eat of it when out of other provision; under the same circumstances I ate muskrats.

Another change in my diet was, when I had gone into the mountains with them to attend an Indian fandango. We were caught in a heavy snow storm. and run out of grub; then we had to turn in on the reserve these people keep to stave off starvation; it is a bread or cake made of dried and powdered grasshoppers and grass seed. It is very good eating, if you have nothing else, and are very, very hungry.

These incidents I mention at this stage of my life as being associated with my first land proprietorship, and after this rather extended parenthesis, now resume the thread of my story.

The last misfortune with my team and many previous mishaps which rendered profit uncertain and heavy expenses sure, tended to discourage me in trying to gain wealth by hauling freight with a two-horse team, and the day after my arrival at Elko I disposed of all my right, title, stock, goodwill and fixtures as included in and represented by my transportation outfit, coming through the transaction without loss.

Then I went back home, locked up the shanty with a wooden plug, bade farewell, for a time only, as I supposed, to my "lodge in the wilderness," and started out for other scenes and occupation.

CHAPTER XXVII.

SPECULATIONS, STRUGGLES AND SCANT SUCCESS.

When I turned my back upon what I now called "home," and could refer to as "my property," I made my way on foot to Carlin.

There I found no opening for investment of capital, and, being offered the job, I engaged as workman in the construction force of the Central Pacific Railroad.

For two weeks I was employed in the laborious work of raising telegraph poles, and fitting them up, being very often and very literally well up in the world; then, with my usual propensity for getting "thick" with some stranger, I formed a new connection.

Forgetful of my past, dearly paid for lessons, I chummed in with a young man named George Barring, who, like myself, had a few hundred dollars of spare cash, which he was anxious to increase into thousands by the most easy and rapid means that could be devised.

My new friend proposed that we should enter into partnership, and start a wood camp or depot; chop and cord the timber

UP IN THE WORLD.

which stood ready, close at hand, and sell it to the railroad company.

His glowing representations as to the amount of business waiting for us to gather it in, the profits to be gained in the trade, the "millions in it" that he insisted we were losing, soon made me as enthusiastic over the project as himself.

We pitched in, bought axes, engaged a force of choppers, and set to work with a will that mowed and rattled down the timber like a hurricane; but my partner lacked "staying qualities," and when we had cut and stacked about two hundred cords, and were ready

RATTLING THE TIMBER.

for a rush of business, he began to grow discouraged, and to take a gloomy view of our prospects.

I wanted to be tied to no croakers or unwilling workers, and there was nothing left for me, under the circumstances, but to make a "give or take" offer, " buy in or sell out" was the time of day then. He sold out.

By the purchase of Barring's interest I had all the wood trade on my hands I could manage. I gave him the full value of his investment at once, except $160, which I afterwards paid, and held his receipt in full for all claims.

The buying in with him, and the buying of him out completely exhausted my ready cash, and I was like the wheels of the wagon, out of which I had made some of my capital—up to the hub in the mire of poverty, a heavy load forcing me deeper down, and no aid likely to be given me.

I had a big lot of wood on hand, or rather, on the ground of my camp, but I had no team to haul it to a market, or money to purchase animals.

My former resolution, that, when I again found myself beset by a sea of troubles, I would, instead of sitting down and crying, grip hold and try to paddle my own canoe, now came back on me to urge me to action, and studying to think of a place where I could go and earn money to buy a team I concluded that I was likely to do best at Elko.

Back to that Station I made my way, and through the kind influences of Mr. James F., now or lately Station Agent at Ogden, Utah Territory, I obtained a situation as Police and Watchman, in which capacity I served until, after six months of such employ, close economy, and scant living, I had saved, from my pay of three dollars per day, the sum of $300. Then I was off again.

"Now," thought I, " get back to the wood camp, purchase a team, go to selling wood, 'like sixty,' and make money hand over fist, that's your game, old man ! "

But when I reached the scene of my cutting, I found that certain dishonest persons had drawn upon my stacks until they had taken over one hundred cords, and further, that they had become so accustomed to consider this cut and piled timber as having been thus accumulated for their special aid, comfort, and benefit, to be taken by them, free gratis, and for nothing, whenever occasion required, that they were very indignant and prepared to forcibly resist any presumptuous attempt upon my part to repossess myself of my wood or demand payment for what they had used.

To make any move towards assuming proprietorship of those piles of wood was equivalent to a declaration of war between one man and all the thieving portion of that community, and that class had the best of me "by a large majority."

The only redress or revenge I could then obtain, in that country and day, was to shoot the parties when I caught them stealing my wood, and on two occasions I did detect them.

But I argued : first, that they might shoot as well and quick, or better and quicker than I could, and a bullet in my body was a poor substitute for cash in my pocket, or wood in the yard ; second, if I did kill one of the robbers, it would be "just my luck " to be sent the same road by some of his friends, or, escaping this, to be gobbled and hung or shut up in the penitentiary for a term of years of my lifetime, and I could not see that a coffin and grave, or board and lodgings, even if furnished without charge, would make me square in my timber transactions.

So I held my fire and my tongue, put the wood speculation down on the well filled profit and loss page of my books, sold what of the wood I could, and left the purchasers to run the risk of getting it, and retired from that decidedly unprofitable business.

CHAPTER XXVIII.

MONEY, MOTHER, AND MATRIMONY.

My little hut at the foot of the hills, "my property,"—"South Fork Farm,"—had still as strong a hold as ever upon my heart.

In my present condition, without occupation and rather disgusted with speculation, my thoughts turned more than ever towards the one spot on earth that I could call "home," and it seemed to me that, for once, interest and inclination both united in directing me to a wise course of proceeding, by prompting my desire to return to the Eden, towards which my feet were aching to point their toes.

I had a good, strong, stand-by friend, a merchant in Elko; to him I went and unburdened my mind, telling him of my doubts, fears, ambitions, hopes and desires.

This kindly merchant not only agreed with me as to the wisdom of settling down to cultivation of my landed estate, but he also offered most substantial proofs of his friendship and confidence in my honesty, as well as the success of my undertaking, by volunteering to provide me with horses, implements, seeds—anything and everything necessary to properly fit my farm out in thorough working order.

I had still some money that had escaped sacrifice in my mania for speculation, and this also aided me in my first attempt as a farmer.

There was still another influence which served to intensify my desire to settle down in life.

My good old mother, who had toiled so hard for me, and whom, my heart told me, I had but illy repaid, had written to me that she desired to come to the United States and live with me. It would have been hard for even her active spirit to have contented itself by "living with me" in the life I had been leading prior to this time, but now I saw my way clear to offer her the shelter of my own roof, and I was impatient to have her with me.

When, therefore, my return to and proper settlement at South Fork Farm was fully arranged for, I sent her word to join me as quickly as possible.

Thinking that I could obtain a double allowance of comfort by one stroke of work, I instructed her to look about, and with a mother's jealous scrutiny, find, select and bring with her a good-looking, hard-working, fair-tempered, honest Danish girl, who was used to farm work, to act as housekeeper, with "a view to matrimony," as the "personal" advertisements of the newspapers put it.

And then I hastened to the farm and busied myself with preparations, and time rolled on, as it always has and will, and the Spring of 1870 arrived, and with the birds and tree buds came the good and most welcome mother, and likewise the prize, picked damsel from Denmark, who looked good enough outside, and was warranted to possess all the old-fashioned, sterling virtues as well as "all the modern improvements"—a perfect *Daisy* to blossom and beautify the entire farm.

Then I felt as though I was really and truly a regular granger, a producer in the land. Cosy and contented under my own vine and fig-tree, with two men to aid me in my agricultural pursuits, the mother and prospective wife keeping all things in apple-pie order in my house. What more could heart desire? "In sweet content, my days are spent," was the song of exceeding gladness I sung in my foolish heart.

I have mentioned, early in this history, that my mother was a woman of most stirring, go-ahead temperament; a Danish-Yankee, or Yankeeish-Dane. When, therefore, she had put my house to rights, combed my wool right smartly to get some of the vagabond kinks and ideas out of it that occasionally cropped up, and bossed everybody into proper running order, the life in that secluded spot became too monotonous for her, and, though she tried to content herself for my sake, she was

"WITH A VIEW TO MATRIMONY."

unhappy, and after a little while she accepted an excellent situation as housekeeper in the stirring town of Elko.

CHAPTER XXIX.

A SQUARE KNOCK DOWN.

The marriage of my Danish importation and self had been often discussed, in all its bearings, between the interested parties in their leisure moments.

Prudence and forethought entered very largely into our confabs and calculations, and it was decided that, before we entered into such a serious and lasting partnership, my worldly success should be insured; so the wedding was postponed until the Fall of the year, when the crops had been gathered and sold.

"IN SWEET CONTENT MY DAYS ARE SPENT!"

Such was the arrangement when my mother left me to go and live at Elko, and the good woman departed content, confident that she had made my calling and election sure.

How true it is that the disposition of events in this world is hardly ever in accordance with the propositions and inclinations of the men and women inhabiting the earth. The eventuation of my calculations at this time only go to prove the soundness of the old Dutchman's proverbial philosophy:

"You purtty surely, most sometimes allvays, shust can't tell, certain fur bosidiv, shust noddings aboud effrydings."

And just so,—you can't!

I was going to raise that crop and sell it, I was going to marry that girl—and with her as my wife, the bright perspective glowed with a long stretch of peace, plenty and continual happiness. I did not raise that crop, consequently I did not sell it. I did not marry that girl, and, consequently, with her as my wife, hand and hand together, we did not journey through life along that pathway illumined by the aforesaid electric light of earthly joy. Not any.

All of which happened in this wise :

It was on the night of August 8th, 1870, that there came to South Fork Farm and its vicinity, entirely uninvited and unwelcome, a bitter, black frost, and it nipped and bit and froze, and in a few dark hours rendered unfit for anything, but turning back into the ground every potato and vegetable I had planted there.

The sight that greeted me when I went out in the morning, told me in a moment the whole story of dire disaster, it was enough to have brought tears into the eyes of the potatoes if the frost had not previously killed them ; it certainly brought the brine into my own, and my heart into my mouth.

I was ruined.

In despair I hurried back into the house and told Mary of the terrible blight which had fallen upon and blasted all our plans, prospects, and potatoes.

Together and in silence we went out to gaze upon the wreck of all our labor, to look upon the scene of desolation. Two heart-broken, forlorn, destitute, overgrown Babes in the Woods, with not even the consoling robins to chirp to and cheer us.

Our misery was too great to find utterance in words, I went into the eye water pumping at once, turning on the full tap ; I sat down and "enjoyed a good cry." Looking up after a time I saw that Mary was also sobbing and weeping as though her heart would break.

The sight of the poor girl's grief aroused my manhood and made me ashamed of my selfish forgetfulness of her.

I tried to console her with words.

" Don't cry over this, my dear," I said, " cheer up and we'll fight it through like men; you and me together, and the Lord will help us in his own way and at his own good time."

My attempt at consolation, my moral reflections, condescending acquiescence in and submission to higher power (when I had no other option) ; my tender tones, and regret at her having to share my misfortunes, did not pan out a cents worth of paying return.

What was it her clear duty to do under such circumstances ?

Plainly to tumble into my arms and rub her nose against my shirt bosom ; to gush out in spasmodic jerks, that she "loved me all the more dearly for the misfortunes that had come upon me ;"—that she would "prefer me in my poverty to the Crown Prince of Denmark, or the eldest son of the President,"— that she would " toil and slave for me," " would die without me," etc., etc.

IDEALITY.

That was the proper and perfectly legitimate stage business for that part of the drama.

Did she do this ? Not much, she didn't.

Oh no ! My Danish Dove wasn't the least "on the gush" so far as I was concerned; she required all her time and attention just then to gush on her own account.

Through all her tears and blubberings, which I was tenderly trying to quench and quiet, she "let me have it."

"She wasn't crying over *my* confounded blasted hopes and *my* misera-

REALITY.

ble, dirty, frost bitten potatoes," she told me ; "it wasn't over *her own* blasted prospects, and the frost bitten flowers of *her* love, for which she had shed those tears."

And she howled louder than ever for a time and then, as if I wasn't stunned enough already, she "hit me agin."

"She could have married a poor man in Denmark, a man whom she always had and always would love ; who was a better and smarter and handsomer man that I ever dared to be ; and she had come over here to marry me and be rich ; and now I was poor, and she didn't love me a cents worth, and never could and never did and never would."

And then she collected all her capacity for howl, and lifted up her voice, and let it out in a manner that it would discourage a fog horn to rival.

I wanted to go somewhere, get into a hole, pull the hole in after me, and thus find an early, peaceful death.

I was worse frost nipped than all the potatoes in and within ten miles around South Fork.

In the course of a considerably checkered career, I had received many hard blows, regular knock downs ; but this was a stiffner, a perfect parali-zation ; this trip-hammer tap that was fired into me by my warranted per-fectly reliable, non-shying, never baulking, imported Danish Filly.

This kicking over of all my matrimonial fat which had been so long simmering, into the hot fire of sudden destruction, drove the loss of crops, prospects, hopes, and all such small matters, clear out of my mind, switched off my train of thought on to another track, and drove it in an entirely different direction.

I am happy to say that I rose equal to the situation. I did not whistle "What shall the harvest be," because I did not then know the dulcet strains of that melody, and I would not have whistled it if I had been ac-quainted with every note of its tooting ; it was unnecessary for me to in-quire what the harvest was going to be, so far as I was concerned, either in the field agricultural or field matrimonial ; I could guess that harvest conundrum, my share of it, first pop, and answer " Nix ! "

111

I think the most unsympathetic of my readers will admit that "things looked blue" for me at this stage of my life's game.

Blue! they were *black!* black as a lump of coal in a dark mine at midnight. I did not think of the old saying that, "when things are at the worst, they must mend," but though "plunged in the depths of deep despair," and howling in a most perfectly natural, unrestrained and justifiable manner, there was an under current of just such philosophy beneath the torrent of thoughts and feelings that swept over my mind and heart.

"Almost twelve years to a day, it is," I exclaimed, as I stood there alone, contemplating the dire ruin about me, "since I first came to America; I have fought fire, struggled through water, endured poverty, abuse, treachery of those I considered friends, suffered sickness, pain, starvation, and undeserved stripes, and now the very elements have conspired to crush me!"

"There are none left to comfort me in this crowning misery. My mother is not here to console, my promised wife has deceived and deserted me, my last coin must go to pay my men; all that remains to me will not pay quarter of my debts; I am a Jonah to good luck.

"Nobody will trust me again for a penny; of food I have not sufficient to live for a week; there is nothing between me and starvation but frostbitten and blackened potato tops and nubbins."

"Mother gone! Mary gone! crops gone! friends and credit gone! hope gone! wits almost gone! empty pockets! empty belly! bare back!"

Boys, *it was a very cold day.*

The undefined feeling that things could not, by any possibility get worse, and a certain amount of the "paddle your own canoe" doctrine that still stuck to me, alone kept me from thoughts of making a third attempt to end my existence.

"Twelve years of bad, bad luck," I said to myself, "it *can't* last, it can't be possible that I am going to suffer such evils for another twelve years, and at the end of that time be in such another fix as this!"

"I'm going to see it out!"

So I just gulped down my sighs, shut my eyes on my sorrows, dried my tears, braced up and faced the music.

I called to the girl who was near by, standing, sulky and ugly.

"Mary," I said to her, "I never tempted you, knowingly, to leave your home and the man you loved. I told my people to tell you all about me before you came over, and since then have given you plenty of chance to learn all about me and my every day life. I have tried faithfully to think of no other girl but you, and to like you and be true to you in every way. Yet all this time you have been carrying deceit in your heart against me. I am more sorry for you than I am for myself."

And in all that I said to her I spoke the truth.

DISGUST.   In all she did she showed   PACK OFF.

her disgust so plainly that I became angry and told her to "pack off."
I write about this serious portion and episode in my life, with
an affectation of now looking only on the comical side of the affair.

I do this because it is far better to so do than indulge in the pathetic
or tragic over misfortunes that can't be helped, and woes that are past
and gone.

But it was a very stiff dose for me just then. Indeed, it was.

CHAPTER XXX.
" NEVER SAY DIE, BOYS ! "

Of course my Mary, who was'nt my Mary, could no longer stay at the
farm under our present agreement to disagree. I had ordered her to leave
but could not thrust her out without a home, so, with some little trouble, I
obtained a place for her at Elko, where she could earn $30 per month.

Though I had little serious care in the girl's future, thinking that she
was calculating enough to look out for herself, I had a certain amount of
interest in the money she made.

Of her own free will she had come from Denmark, with funds furnished by me, under the contract that she should make me a good, true
wife ; the impossibility of her doing this under any circumstances she had
herself made very plain.

Hard pushed as I now was for cash, I did not propose to be the only
loser in the whole transaction ; the shock to my self-conceit and vanity
was beyond remedy or repair, but the financial injury might be very considerably lessened. Sixty dollars, applied in small lots, to my pocket, is
the amount of salve that helped to cure that smarting sore.

The loss of the girl I got quickly over when once I was able to see her
with unglamored eyes. She was not true even to the "poor man whom
she had always loved in the old country ; " never went or tried to go back
to him, though she could easily have done so. She married a stock raiser,
but did not turn out well, as she proved to be lacking in those qualities of
truth that lead to honest dealing in all conditions of life. Let her R.I.P.

After settling my love affairs, which were not love affairs at all, being
foolishness on my part and a swindle on that of the girl, I sought out
again my merchant friend at Elko, and to him told my " plain, unvarnished
tale," with a full statement of my position and prospects, or rather my
lack of the latter.

The jolly dealer condoled with and laughed at me, cheered me up
wonderfully with his kind, pleasant, hopeful advice and way of looking on
the bright side of things.

"Never say die, boy ! Get up and go at it
again ! "

That is what he bade me do, to take courage
and go to work, not to worry about my debts, that
I could pay him when and how I could, and that
he felt I could and would square all up with him
and come out ahead some day.

This was timely, sensible advice and comfort,
and I acted upon it.

MY ELKO FRIEND. Going out to the farm I gathered up all I

113

could, salvage from the wreck, and with my team I hauled wood and sold it to whoever wanted to buy.

HAULING OUT OF DEBT.

A neighbor had very considerable confidence in my ability to get out of scrapes, and he loaned me $200, taking my farm as security.

The money borrowed from neighbor John, I paid to my kind helping friend in Elko, and what I made in selling wood I used to pay up other debts; then I transferred my team to my mother for employment under her direction and abandoned my unfortunate property and all thoughts of being a farmer.

Having thus disposed of most of my goods and chattels, mortgaged my farm, (and I never raised the mortgage or anything else off it), satisfied all creditors who wouldn't or couldn't afford to wait, I put myself inside of a new suit of clothes presented by my steadfast Elko creditor, and broke out once more into the world.

I drifted on, hunting fortune in every promising locality, but finding poor pickings until I reached Ogden Station, Utah Territory; there I struck a "pay streek," as the miners call it, by being again employed on police and watchman duty by the railroad company.

My wages were good and pay prompt; quickly as I earned money I remitted it my Elko friend to pay off the balance due him and sundry debts to others. I spent little or nothing for myself, except to procure what I absolutely required.

A few months only of this life and I felt like a new man. I had a well paid position, knew my employers were satisfied with me; was free of debt, free of care, free

RE-FITTED. of sorrow, and free of a girl who would have married me when she cared nothing for me, because she thought I had a little money.

What big blessing cropped up from those frost bitten potatoes.

We just can't always tell, "What will the harvest be."

CHAPTER XXXI.
ON THE PLATFORM AT OGDEN.

I was mighty well fixed at Ogden; there were certain well understood and plain duties to be performed, and so that these were properly executed I was allowed to choose my own ways and means of effecting them.

On the arrival of trains on the Union Pacific line, Ogden being its terminus, I had to attend to transferring the passengers whose route was still further to the cars of the Central Pacific Road. Here the smattering I had of many languages served me well, and I collected gossip from almost every corner of the earth through the medium of the many emigrants coming under my notice and questionings.

I blundered into this well paid position by what I at first considered a side lick·from my old ill luck.

When I first arrived there and was taken on by the company, I was carried on the roll of the car superintendent, and all the rolling stock arriving and standing over at that station was my charge. I had to go through the cars, look after their condition, lock them at night, etc.

The boss under whom I then served was, one night, discovered by me in strange company in the car under circumstances which were plainly no part of his duty. I should certainly have held my tongue about the matter, but he seemed to think it necessary to take time by the forelock and try to muzzle me. The day after my discovery of the gentleman in *flagrante delicto* I received my discharge through his hands.

Not feeling disposed to be bounced in so summary a manner, I reported all the facts and results as far as they affected me, to the station superintendent, James Campbell, and awaited action from higher authority. In a few days a decision was rendered, my former boss was shipped, I was re-employed and given a position as station or platform police.

A GUARDIAN ANGEL.

From the time of the ill luck that turned out to be good luck, the current of my fortunes seemed to change.

I was now master of transfer, looking after all the emigrants. Daily and hourly were incidents occurring in my life, but I can only mention a few here.

The railroad station was much frequented by gamblers, ticket scalpers, swindlers of every degree and "bad men" generally. It was my business to keep these gentleman away from the depot and its regular legitimate patrons, and I adopted all manner of expedients to do so, using force only when necessary.

There was one scalper, who by pleasant treatment sometimes, and again by threats, I had controlled for quite a time ; he was called "Big Steve," and was a perfect specimen of the Western rough, over seven feet high, and "a shooter."

Steve and I got along with average amiability, until one day, when he had gotten outside of too much tangle foot, crazy head whiskey, he concluded to come to an understanding with me.

I was informed that "Big Steve is looking for you and swears he will not be bluffed off the platform any longer by that big Dutchman."

And sure enough, I soon spied my man howling drunk, with pistol in hand and mouth full of curses, at one end of the long platform.

Dropping between two lines of cars, I made my way under their cover, until I got near to him and took up position where my body was well covered by a pile of boxes and trunks.

Soon he came up directly in front of where I was secreted, and much to his dismay he was "fetched up, all standing," with my six-shooter pointing directly at his face, while my own arm and head projected from behind the baggage barricade.

"Throw down that pistol and put up your hands!" I shouted.

Steve was staggered by that sight worse than by his whiskey, but he could do nothing. I "had the drop on him," and he obeyed orders.

That finally settled Big Steve, he was quiet as a lamb ever after with me. The lessee of the depot restaurant for the interest I always manifested for the good of his establishment made me

"PUT UP YOUR HANDS!"

welcome to my board, which was very welcome to me, and the "run of the place."

He employed many men, and I was convinced that some of them robbed him of provisions he bought to use in his business; such also was his opinion. I watched certain of his employees until I had caught them "dead to rights," and took them with their plunder before their master. This caused these men to become my enemies, and they vowed to drive me away.

In accordance with such resolution, three of them, coats off and sleeves rolled up, came up to me and announced their intentions of giving me, first, an unmerciful thrashing, and second, notice to quit.

I took Western methods of meeting the question.

With revolver at full cock and arms length, I backed into a secure position and opened parley.

"Look here," said I, "you want me to apologize to you for doing my duty, to take a licking, and to get out."

"That's just what you got to do" answered their spokesman.

"And that's just what I aintgoing to do, nary one of the three" said I.

"If you had come one at a time I'd have given you a chance to get even, but now I'm going to ask you a question, which one of you wants to die first, for the one that steps another pace forward will get the roof of his head blowed off. Do you hear me!"

These fellows were all Mormons, and believed that when they died they would go straight to glory and Joe Smith, but they didn't want to pay a visit to Smith just then, and they backed out and left me alone ever after so far as regarded violence.

But they "had me up" before a Mormon Alderman, Walter Thompson, and on the oath of three Mormon cowards this Mormon "Justice" dispensed "Mormon Justice" to me, fining me $25 and costs for flourishing a deadly weapon and threatening the lives of several valuable citizens, as he called these fellows.

He also bound me over in bail of $200 to keep the peace for one year. I did not wish to ask anyone to become my bondsman, and having a lot of mining stock, wildcat and worthless, I offered to deposit this with him as security in lieu of bail. He took it and the scrip proved of more value to me in that way than I ever expected it to be in any manner.

On another occasion I came near getting into much more serious trouble through over zealous and hasty exercise of my police functions. One day a gentleman with his family, including a well grown young lady, alighted from the California train.

Before the arrival of the cars a carriage had drawn up near to the station and a young man who had come in it was walking about the platform.

This young man hurried to the just arrived young lady, seized her and her satchel, rushed to the carriage, both were bundled in, the driver whipped up his horses and away they went.

The old gentleman and remainder of his family were frantic; like Shylock of old, he shouted,

"My daughter, my money!"

"They have stolen my daughter! Stop them! Stop them! I'll give a thousand dollars to whoever will stop them." My duty and interest both prompted me to put my best foot forward and work for glory, money, and the preservation of the law.

I travelled after that carriage at a lively rate, by cutting through mud piles and across lots. I intercepted the vehicle and ordered them to

halt, and, on no attention being paid to my summons, I sent two shots flying into the top of the carriage with the full intention of hurting somebody, for I firmly believed that a violent abduction and robbery was being carried out.

The team soon left me behind and when I next caught up with it the horses

BY DUTY, VIRTUE, AND CASH INCITED. were standing before the house of a Mormon Bishop, and inside the young man, with the perfectly willing young lady were being married as fast as words could join them.

An Ogden policeman, stationed at the door, told me I had better go back where I belonged, and I had just made up my mind that the job had been "put-up" beforehand and very nicely carried out when papa, mamma, and the rest came panting and puffing to the spot.

The sight of the old gentleman put me in mind of the promised reward and I delicately hinted that though I was not entitled to the full thousand dollars promised, I thought three hundred would be a fair proportion for my efforts to carry out his desires and my success in running the party down.

The unappreciative Californian reviled me in very strong language and called me all sorts of names for trying, as he said, my "best to shoot his daughter."

I was forced to return to the station with, to use a common simile, "my tail between my legs," minus any reward but the consciousness of having tried to do my duty, and to endure the laugh that all hands kept up, long and loud, at my expense.

For the tramps that passed my way, and many they were who hobbled up to that platform, I had a fraternal tenderness which even the stern demands of duty could not altogether suppress.

It was "a cold day" for the "hoofer" when he did not transfer a quarter from my pocket to his own dirty fist, and under all circumstances he received a square fill up from the broken scraps I could always obtain at the restaurant.

From one end of the line to the other the tramps on that route knew Big Dutch Hans, the Policeman of Ogden Station, and swore unanimously that he was a "jolly good fellow, safe for a quarter or square meal anytime."

One of this ignoble Brotherhood got the best of me and taught me a lesson in my old "profession" which is too good to pass over in my reminiscences.

He was a fellow countryman, another wandering Dane, and a most pitiful object when I first spied him, hollow, ragged, limping, and bare-footed, my heart went out to him.

I took him in and fed him, got him to clean himself as much as his principles would allow him to indulge in such performance, took off my feet and gave him the good, almost new, boots I had on, I contenting myself for the time with an old pair I had at the Depot ; and, in his case, I increased my cash donation to the sum of $1.

The food had braced him up, the slight washing he gave himself (only to oblige me) proved that he had a white skin underneath all its covering of dirt, the boots enabled him to step out firmly.

But the cash ! The cash transmogrified him entirely; he was a new man throughout. Immediately he began to patronize me, asked me over to take a drink (to be paid for with my money) with an air of condescension which plainly said, "you see I ain't too proud to drink with you even if you are only a common policeman," and then waving me a lordly adieu he started into Ogden.

GIVING MY BOOTS.

A few hours later I saw my tramp returning, my dollar was inside his skin in the shape of whiskey, likewise also two more dollars worth of the same commodity was in the same "tank," that sum having been realized by him from the sale of *my* boots to a Mormon who had a keen eye for a good bargain.

Not drunk was my tramp, three dollars worth of even Utah whiskey

GETTING A BLAST.

could not "fetch him that way," but he felt good, and when he halted his bare feet before me, and I indignantly asked, " Where are my boots, what have you done with them," he cooly replied,

" Sold 'em of course, old cock ! Why what a bloomin' fool you must be to think I could go beggin' an' git anything with a pair o' boots like them on."

" By-by, Bobby, see you later; " he waved me a farewell and was off.

. This is one of the charities I regret having bestowed, but I had about that much fun over the fellow's impudence, and life was going too easy with me those times for me to worry over trifles.

CHAPTER XXXII.
COPIOUS, CURIOUS, COMICAL, COURTSHIPS.

I was so pleasantly fixed at Ogden, so well contented and so over-stocked with blessings, that I began to feel as though I had more than my share, and I cast about for a partner with whom to divide my joys.

The old saying that "Fools rush in where angels fear to tread," is continually verified when the matrimonial fever gets hold of a likely subject.

Spite of my unlucky speculations in that line, or unfortunate attempt to enter into it, I was prepared to endorse the scriptural doctrine that it " is not good for man to be alone;" and I was impatient to get into double harness.

I was surrounded by people of the Mormon faith, and many were the efforts made, not exactly to convert me, for, as I was nothing in a creed sense, I could not be converted ; but to bring me into the Mormon fold, to initiate me into the first mysteries, so that in time I could develop into a full blown saint with any number of wives I desired.

I " couldn't see it." Somehow, there was a kind of "strongness " about the Mormon doctrines and practices that, when it was proposed that I should swallow them whole, rendered me of the opinion that they were too rich for my stomach, and I steadily refused to take the pill even though it was sometimes offered with a very nice sugar coating.

Matrimonially inclined, however, I was and I kept my "whether eye" open for the right craft to come sailing along, when I determined to board and compel her surrender at all hazards.

There was a certain buxom, good natured widow, No. 4 of a Mormon bishop, to whose charms and very substantial attractions I gave serious consideration for some time. This widow, who had been the proud one-quarter wife of a now departed saint, was willing to become Mrs. Hans Lykkejæger, and to bestow upon me herself, two children, and sundry worldly goods, house, cattle, etc., which would have quite set me up in the world, but she insisted that I should "pass through the water," in other words, be baptized in and become a disciple of the Mormon Church.

I wasn't willing to "go through the water" for the widow and, as the sporting papers say, "the match was declared off."

And I kept looking around. Many were the fine girls I had joking confabs with as I met them in the trains or at the depot, when, in discharge of my police duties I had to see that they were properly started for their destinations, and it often entered my mind that in one of these encounters I should find my fate. "We met by chance," can be sung with truth. by more loving couples than most people fancy.

Though continually I saw hundreds of pretty faces that were pleasant to look upon, yet I never got a square call, until one day, passing through the train as usual, I spied, sitting quietly by the window, a clear skinned, rosy cheeked, big, bright, honest eyed, plump young girl, good looking as to looks, and looking good as to mental and moral attributes, strength,

MASHED.

GRETA.

health, grace and modesty, were shown in every movement and intelligence in every feature.

The one-quarter wife, and now widow of the departed bishop, was knocked out of mind completely.

I was dead gone, "mashed."

I "went for" that quiet damsel who was setting so demurely at the car window just "saying nothing to nobody."

My official station of course permitted me to enter into conversation with her, without the least appearance of impertinence on my part, or impropriety on hers.

"Where are you going?" I asked, I did not then know that I was repeating the first words of an old English song, or I might have added the balance and said, "My pretty maid!"

My official dignity, my evident desire to please and attract her attention, and the well displayed personal charms which my bulky body made prominent, neither dismayed, overawed or fascinated the quiet young lady; nor did she seem to be the least inclined to cultivate my acquaintance.

I had addressed her in English, and in answer received a decidedly short:

"Nix verstach!"

"Oh," said I, "I see you are a German."

Now the Germans are not liked by some nations of this earth, and the country from which this maiden came was one where they are particularly detested.

"No, I am not," was fired at me very sharp, with much emphasis on the "No" and the "Not;" and then she added:

"I am a native of Denmark."

And I crowed! here was luck; tons of it!

Quickly I claimed my rights as a fellow countryman, and in the pleasure of meeting a stranger who could speak her mother's tongue, the pretty maid relaxed somewhat in her stern guardedness of demeanor.

"She was going to join her brother in California," she told me.

I flew around like an old hen with only one chicken, got her coffee, water, dinner, anything and everything, and I made as big a fool of myself generally, as men always do under such circumstances, and women never.

During the time that elapsed before the train started I was enabled to have considerable chat with Greta as I shall now call her.

At last I grew sufficiently bold to ask her if she could not be induced to stop in Ogden and keep house for me.

My answer came quickly.

"No, sir, I don't know you or anything about you. You and your town are alike strange to me, and you are too young a man for any girl to serve in the capacity of housekeeper."

Then I came out with the truth and told her I was looking for a housekeeper who would, by matrimonial contract, be joint partner and houseowner, and I pressed my suit with all the powers of fascination and language that I possessed.

But Miss Greta sat unmoved by my eloquence and remained immovable in every sense until the train moved her onward in her journey.

I had gotten in the station an envelope addressed to myself and properly stamped, under pretence of anxiety to learn that my fair country woman had arrived safely at her destination. I asked her to take it, and when she reached her brother's home, to please enclose a few lines announcing such fact, and drop the letter in the post-office for me.

She didn't make any rash promises one way or the other, but she took the envelope.

Then I chuckled over my sly proceedings, and thought what a sharp fellow I was to thus lay the foundation of a correspondence with my pretty, innocent, unsuspecting little Danish Greta.

Just as if she didn't know the meaning every move I made, and laugh at me for a clumsy blunderer to boot!

Well, she was " gone from my gaze like a beautiful star," and though I thought of her very often, and wondered and hoped that I should hear from, perhaps see her, yet my passion did not cause me to neglect my business, meals, or the steady prosecution of another little courting match I had on hand at that time.

There was a certain Mormon, and he had a little wife ; and the little wife had a good lump of a saucy sister named Sally, and I had been " sparking " Sally most industriously with fair success for some months."

A bird in the hand is worth a whole flock on an unknown brother's farm away off in California, so I did not cut loose from Sally by any means.

The Mormon brother-in-law of Miss Sally desired to cultivate a still closer relationship with the fair one, he destined her to become wife No. 2, and wife who was No. 1, and at 'this time the only one, earnestly desired that I should marry her sister and thus remove temptation from the way of her fickle and over matrimonially inclined husband.

Sally also preferred to be the first and all in her married life, so she and the lady of the house always made me welcome, and I took care to give the Mormon Boss no chance to carry out his desires towards me as indicated by his black looks when we met.

It was about six weeks after I had met and, all too soon, parted with Greta, when back came my envelope, and in it a few simple words, telling me of her safe arrival and thanking me for attentions bestowed.

Then I chuckled again, and spent time, ink, and brains in my very best attempt at penmanship, composition, courtesy, and blarney in answering the dear little note.

To this I got a reply, and I answered that.

Then I got another reply, and I answered that.

And each answer I wrote was longer and stronger and sweeter and more " taffyish " than the one preceding, and at last they grew so red hot that it's a wonder they didn't burn up the U. S. Mail, cars, agents, post offices, and all.

I proposed to Greta to come to Ogden and be my wife.

And she wrote me back that I should send her the money to come on and she would do so.

Glory Hallelujah!

But then in crept the gloomy devil of distrust, and I began to think I had been too fast. I argued in my newly found timidity and caution:

" Maybe the girl ain't so innocent as she looks, there's no such thing as knowing these girls, maybe she is going to get the fifty dollars I will send to bring her on, and then she, her brother, and some beau will laugh at Big Fool Hans, and the way they have made him pay for his blundering conceit."

And so I made an extra double fool of myself by concocting what I thought was a very good plan.

I wrote to her and sent her an order, which on her presentation of it at the railroad office near her brother's home, would secure a ticket for passage in an emigrant train to Ogden. To the railroad agent at the place mentioned I sent instructions to supply such a ticket to such a person as I described when she presented her order for it, and that payment therefor would be made by the station master at Ogden.

Then I chuckled again at my cuteness, and I kept on chuckling, and presently a reply to my last letter was placed in my hands by the post office clerk.

"If, after asking me to be your wife and helpmate through life, after all the professions of affections you have made, and all the expressions of reliance you have written ; if, after all these you have so little trust in me that you refuse to keep your promise and send to me direct the money you offered to pay my passage to Ogden, and have to depend upon my going to exhibit myself before station masters in order to get a ticket ; and if, after all your liberal offers to support me in comfort, you can only send for your much sought wife that is to be, to come to you in a rough, greasy, emigrant's car, you can find some other wife than me, and as you place more

BEFORE READING.

I'VE GOT MY LETTER.

AFTER READING.

I'VE GOT THE SACK.

dependence on the railroad company than on my honor, I guess you had better marry the railroad company for you will never marry Greta."

These were not of course the actual words used, but the above was the tenor and about the tune, and it "knocked me stiff."

I didn't chuckle so much then, I went out and, in a figurative sense I kicked myself until I was black and blue.

I loved the girl ten times more now that she had refused me, almost called me a fool, intimated that I was one, and proved that I was one, than I did before.

I wanted to write and explain, but in her letter she told me that she should never take a line from me again, and also, that she was going to leave her brother's house and go elsewhere.

So I had lost her, and it served me right.

But I went all the same, and put on double pressure in my courtship of sally.

CHAPTER XXXIII.

A PERPLEXED POLICEMAN.

I courted the fair Sally with frequency and zeal after the set back I received from the Danish girl I had seen so little of, thought so much about, and from whom I got such a stunning back-hander.

And Sally took very kindly to the courting. She was young, plump, smart—just the least bit tart in temper, with a dash of pepper and vinegar in her composition, which added spice to the sparking ; though they might have proved rather too high seasoning as a regular diet.

I had been cultivating Sally before I ever laid eyes on Danish Greta ; partly because Sally pleased me, because I was made welcome and comfortable when I called, by both of the sisters, married and single, and because it spited the brother-in-law who wanted to be husband-in-fact, to see me coming there.

Though Sally and I were so "thick" that the old gossips said "Big Hans was going to marry that Sal. Higgins, or if he didn't he'd orter; and she'd hook him, sure as shootin," and though I was careful not to tell her of my encounter with the beauty of the cars, yet I had not actually in my own opinion, committed myself and would never have done so had not the message from California blasted all my hopes in that direction.

I knew that I had made a fool of myself, and with the weakness of human nature, I wanted to make a fool. of somebody else and so I redoubled my attentions to Sally and she was evidently expecting, at my every visit, to receive an invitation to become Mrs. Platform Police ; and I must acknowledge that so far as actions went, she had a fair right to expect such solicitation from me.

I used often, during the spare hours (I was my own master between the arrival of trains), to run up and do a little extra sweethearting—courting between courtings, as it were ; and sometimes, through carelessness on my part, a general free-and-easy way we had of " slopping around" out there, or some extra dusty work about the depot ; I would make a call upon the beauty in working clothes that were decidedly the worse for wear and would have been much better for brushing.

The damsel felt so certain of her coming promotion ; so sure that she would soon be sole proprietress of my heart and home, that she began to assume some of the privileges of such ownership, and especially objected to my occasional decidedly soiled appearance.

" I wish, Mr. Lykkejæger," she said, one day : "that you were more careful of your appearance, if not out of respect for yourself, then through the consideration you express for me."

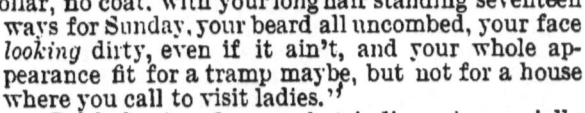

" You come up here to see me, with your breeches in your boots, and dirty, torn shirt, no collar, no coat, with your long hair standing seventeen ways for Sunday, your beard all uncombed, your face *looking* dirty, even if it ain't, and your whole appearance fit for a tramp maybe, but not for a house where you call to visit ladies."

SAUCY SALLY.

I felt hurt and somewhat indignant, especially as this was a case somewhat of "pot calling kettle black," for Miss Sally, though never what might be called actually slovenly, was yet so prone to *en deshabille* in her working hours, that " carelessness " was a very mild word whereby to express her style. When "prinked up" she was a tight, trim craft, other times, " dowdy " is about the figure of it.

I made no answer to Miss Sally at the time of her remonstrance or rebuke, the principal reason being that I had none handy to return. I thought of several very cutting things I might have said in reply, but as these sharp shots did not occur to me for some days, and after long consideration, they hardly seemed worth firing off and I waited for a chance to get square.

My mind works slowly—all great bodies do.

But still I stuck to Sally, and she cottoned to me and her market was, to all intents, made ; the final words only being wanting to close the bargain. For bargain it was more than anything else and we both knew it, though the love-making went on as though it was real.

This was the state of affairs, when, one fine morning, a letter bearing a strange post-mark was put in my hands. It was from Greta.

With a few plain words she stated her object in writing ; she said that her brother and his people, with whom she had before lived, and who knew of her meeting with, and letters from me, had written her that there was a letter in their possession which they were sure was from me, but they would not forward it to her. She thought, and correctly, that they only wrote this to tease her, and she wanted to be sure about it, so she penned her inquiry to me.

This pen and ink communication from the object of my dreams, sent the smouldering flames of love again into active blaze and my blue-shirted bosom covered a regular barbecue bon-fire.

I answered that letter by return of mail, explaining that, rough as I was, I had too much good breeding and self-respect, to have ever written a line to a young lady who so decidedly forbade me so to do, and whom I had so seriously, though unintentionally offended.

The amount of remorse, hope, fear, explanation, expostulation, desperation, solicitation, admiration, and every other 'ation, I or any one else ever thought of, that I put in this and subsequent letters (for the correspondence was renewed and waxed extensive), need not be recalled or recited here. The reader may, probably does know "just how it is," himself or herself.

To make a long story a short one, the course of true love was taken up where it had been dropped, the break nicely joined with " soft sawder," all rough places smoothed over, and Greta promised to come to me if I sent for her.

She said nothing about the kind of ticket or mode of travelling ; she had given me a liberal education on that point, in one written lesson.

Overjoyed, I certainly was, proud and almost happy ; not entirely serene, however, for there was one fly buzzing about the sweetmeats of my coming feast of the soul. It was Sally. What would *she* say, and worse yet, what would she *do?* I " felt goose-flesh all over me " when I thought of Sally.

Through total loss of knowledge, and lack of invention, how to act, I postponed making any decrease in my attentions to Sally, and gave her no intimation of the change in my matrimonial plans until the very last moment.

It would have walked into a hundred dollars and left a very large gap, to have bought the ticket for Greta to come, in style, from her place of residence to Ogden, and, if that amount could be saved, it would do much towards fitting up with household comforts.

So I wrote to the Assistant General Superintendent of the road, who knew me well, and, after dilating upon my long, faithful, and invaluable services for the Company, I told of my coming marriage, explained that, in order to prevent the Railroad from being crippled by my absence from my post, the lady had consented to come to me, and that I wanted, asked for, and thought I ought to have a free ticket for her use. All of which the Station Master at Ogden endorsed as " O.K." and "approved," and forwarded the document to headquarters.

I got the pass, sent it to Greta, and was notified of the day, hour, and train in which to expect her.

And yet I was not happy. There was Sally !

I received a dispatch, Greta had started, would be there on time ; that meant the next day.

Did you ever hear " It is best to be off with the old love before you are on with the new ; " I never had listened to the proverb but I felt it in my BONES.

There was Sally Higgins !

That's what was the matter with me.

CHAPTER XXXIV.

ALL O. K.

There was just about twenty-four hours left for me to fight a grand battle with Fate and Sally Higgins.

The moment I was at leisure for a few hours I directed my footsteps towards the scene of the pending conflict.

Fortune favored me, accident suggested cause, despair gave way to inspiration.

As I drew near to the home of the maiden whose fair hopes I so ruthlessly proposed to forever extinguish, I beheld the lady, all unconscious of my presence, in a very loose wrapper, very big and slippy slippers, with milk pail on arm, skirts held very high, picking her way over the barn yard towards the cow shed.

The shapely " continuations " no longer appeared as models of grace and beauty in my eyes, the stockings seemed loose and baggy, were evidently not over clean, and from each base and rear of these foot coverings bulged, in full sight and development, a round, red, rosy, bare heel.

I was disgusted as I compared this slatternly sight with a mental picture of the trim, neat little woman that was travelling in the direction of my home and arms, and I wondered " how I could ever have thought that Sally Higgins would suit me."

Such is life—and men.

I came to a right about, hurried into Ogden, and put in execution an idea suggested by those tattered stockings and the spur of necessity.

Fixing myself up in " go-to-meeting " style, which meant putting on cleaner and better clothes than usual, I went to the largest store in the place and purchased one dozen ladies' stockings of excellent quality.

From every pair of these, except one to put on top of the lot in the box, I carefully cut out the heels.

Then, white-shirted and shaved, I sought Sally.

I was welcomed to the house, and, after a little time, spent in fixing up, the lady appeared in the room where I was awaiting her.

The weather had been discussed and skirmishers of conversation thrown out, when, after a time, I brought my masked guns into position.

With many explanations and assurances that I had no intention of taking any undue liberty, I presented the offering I had brought.

"Don't apologize, Mr. Lykkejæger," answered pleased Miss Sally, as she took the well wrapped up package.

"We know each other well enough to allow of some slight deviation from strict rules. Anyhow, I always did think that if a gentleman thought anything of a lady, it showed more sense on his part to give her something that would be serviceable and lasting, than to be spending money for useless trinkets or perishable articles. The stockings are *just* what I wanted and I'm a thousand times obliged to you."

"Hem! Yes! Just so!" said I, "I rather thought you *did* want stockings, and so I selected them as a present. I do not know if I got the right size, but you can easily see."

"Oh yes, just wait a moment," and she hopped out to the kitchen to inspect the gift, to show her sister, and I doubt not, to conclude that the final words were now to be spoken; naturally she thought so, for when it comes to giving stockings for presents, things must be pretty well to a head—or heel.

During the few moments of her absence, I was in a quandry, whether to cut and run before her return or wait and "see it out." I looked for and laid handy my hat; I put the door wide open, I assured myself that the dog was chained up and that the men were all away at work; I counted how many steps would take me into the high road—I had my line of retreat all planned out and open, so I waited.

But not long, Sally was back in a very few moments, a pair of stockings in each fist, and ten pairs more, with only one pair of heels in the lot, over her arms and shoulders. She didn't quite know how to take in the situation yet, and her action and speech were undecided.

"Why, look here!" she said, "what does this mean? there's some mistake; the people at the store must have been giving you damaged goods, there's only one pair of these stockings that have heels in them."

I grabbed my hat, stood on my feet, took another look to be certain that all was clear for a run.

"Miss Sally, I am aware that you have very decided opinions in regard to dress and personal appearances; more than once you have rated me on my neglect and want of propriety in appearing before you in my working clothes. You hurt my feelings, but I said nothing. This morning, I wandered up this way to make an early call upon you. I saw you crossing the yard; you did not see me, your high held dress and

THE STOCKINGS GET ME "THE MITTEN."

your low heeled slippers enabled me to study carefully the peculiarities of each foot covering. I thought that either from economy or for purposes of ventilation you had adopted heelless stockings from choice, for such sections were certainly not in either of those articles of which I had such an extensive view this morning. This is why I amputated those I bought for you.

The amazement of the girl rendered her speechless for the time it took me to shoot off my little speech.

But she wasn't speechless very long, not very.

I have remarked before that Sally had a temper ; she showed then that she had not lost any of it, that she had a more than ample stock on hand and on tongue equal to any and all demands, and she drew upon it in the most liberal way to pay me for the "outrage," "insult," "brutality," etc., etc.

I can't, I really can't, do the matter justice. I can't just remember what she did and what she didn't say. There was a mixture of red-peppers, vitriol, nitro-glycerine, red-hot pokers, tears, tongue-lashings, reproaches, threats, bad-names, scalding water, blazing-eyes, flying finger-nails. erupting volcanoes, spouting geysers, and cyclonious blizzards, and stockings that defies description—I give it up.

She gave me up. She told me to go, never to return. That was what I wanted her to tell me; that was what I was hunting for ; the balance of what she told me I received as verbal embroideries, embellishments, and figures of speech, incident, but not material to the "sack" I was anxious she should give me.

Hat in hand, hand on door knob, I bowed my adieu.

"I wish you a very good day, Miss Sallie, and a good-bye also."

And I skipped.

CHAPTER XXXV.
GOOD.

Greta came.

All smiles, plumpness, health, beauty, truthful frankness, and trusting innocence, she came.

And then I was happy.

I had arranged that her comforts on the journey should be attended to and provided for, by communicating with parties at the different stations on the route, and good nature, with curiosity to see the girl who was coming to marry Big Hans, made all my friends along the road very prompt in seeking her out.

I may say here, that, though I was in receipt of a very considerable salary and by some private speculations and mercantile ventures increased my income, yet, payment of back debts, as before mentioned, had kept me comparatively poor, and would continue to do so for some time to come.

I had written all this to Greta, told her honestly how I was fixed and how little we would have at first.

I make this explanation to show that my sweetheart then, my wife now, did not marry me from cool, calculating, mercenary motives. Whether I was "all her fancy painted me" or not, she had made up her mind that I was a man she could love and trust, and she married me from love and took me on trust.

Her reply to my confession of poverty was that she had decided and promised to marry me and she would keep her word.

"If we have no bed, we can sleep on the floor."

"If we have no chairs we can sit on boxes."

"If we have no butter, we can eat dry bread, and sweeten it with the conserve of content."

That's what my true hearted Danish girl wrote me.

Hadn't I struck luck?

CHAPTER XXXVI.

BETTER.

On her arrival I took Greta to the house of an elderly lady friend, and we had a long talk over our plans and hopes for the future.

When she had somewhat rested, I proposed that she should take a short walk and see the town.

Together we went out and sauntered through the streets, a very well contented and much looked after couple.

As we walked and chatted, I spied a well known, short, neatly dressed gentleman approaching us.

"My girl," I said, "what did you come here for?"

"Don't you know?" was the reply.

"Shall we get married?" I asked.

"Please yourself and you'll please me," I got in answer.

"There's a gentleman coming, over there, who can tie us up that way," said I; "he's the Methodist minister."

"All right," said Greta.

That settled it.

So I crossed the road and accosted the parson, told him my sweetheart had come on, that we intended to get married, might as well do it at once, and wanted him to do the job.

"I'm just going down to the butcher's to get some meat for dinner," said he. I'll be home in half an hour, will that suit you?"

"Exactly," said I.

So I went back to Greta, took her to the widow's house again, and, while the minister went to get his meat, I made my arrangements to have "my hash settled."

My own preparations were simple, inexpensive and hurried.

With that perfectly excusable and all womanly desire for proper wedding fixings, Greta had all her "things" prepared for the momentous occasion, her baggage was hurried up to the landlady's house, and from the trunk was taken all the "trotting harness" and paraphernalia peculiar to and necessary for the event, and on my return I found my demure little grub transmogrified into a most gorgeous butterfly, blooming and blushing, sweet and spreading, rosy and ready.

I bought a paper collar, a pair of cuffs of the same material, articles of apparel to which I was little used; astonished and improved my boots by a "shine," gave an extra hist to my breeches, by taking a reef in my suspenders; my coat was rather short, and the rear section of my pantaloons might have been in better repair; and my wedding costume was complete.

Greta and I were at the minister's "on time."

The parson did not seem the least excited, or to view the occasion as in any way extraordinary. That appeared queer to me.

I was in a cold sweat, yet hot, red faced, puffing like a porpoise, and worse scared, I didn't know at what, than I ever was in battle or fight. But I didn't think of running away.

A housemaid and school-marm were two ready, interested, and sympathetic witnesses.

The Minister stood up.

We did ditto.

It didn't take much longer, and was far more pleasant than tooth pulling.

I was married.

AT LAST.

CHAPTER XXXVII.
BEST—AND LAST.

Mrs. and Mr. Hans Lykkejæger!

The newly-wedded couple received barrels and barrels of congratulations and good wishes ; a very short string could have tied up in a bundle all the presents.

Neither congratulations or gifts came from Miss Sally Higgins. That young lady formed the exception to be found in every general rule.

I have stated that I made some outside mercantile ventures. A gentleman in California had been for months sending me consignments of produce from that State. He came to Ogden, and said:

"Look here, Hans! you're married now and got to look ahead. Do you propose to work all your life as a railroad servant, or do you want to strike out and make something of and for yourself ? "

" But I ain't got any money," said I.

" I'll tell you what I'll do," spoke up my friend, "I'll let you have two thousand dollars' worth of goods on sale; you'll soon build up a trade and be independent of the world."

Though I had been successful in my small dealings while at Ogden, yet I doubted my ability to transact trade regularly, my former experiments and experiences in that line had rendered me cautious.

"But I ain't got any money," I repeated.

"Money be blowed!" said my sanguine Californian, "if you have two thousand dollars' worth of goods, and can't get store-room and all else without money, you ain't the man I took you for!"

So I consulted with Mrs. L. I always did and always will consult Mrs. L., and she never gives wrong advice.

The offer was duly and carefully discussed and weighed, pro and con. There was the giving up of a perfect certainty, in good wages and steady employment, for a very uncertain embarkation in trade, and trade had always floored me.

But I had a partner now, with brave heart, cool head and willing hands.

"Nothing venture, nothing gain." Trade won.

I said good-bye to the Platform and the Central Pacific Railroad with regret. My luck had turned from the moment I became connected with it. I had found there the hole for which I was the *peg*. I had been treated fairly, generously, and like a man, by every prominent official connected with it. They were all practical men, every one of them, and they were keen to recognize and anxious to reward zeal in their service.

The Central Pacific Railroad was the conception, and its building the work of self-made AMERICAN MEN. I cannot take space to mention particularly and by name all I would like to, but as a representative of all I take Mr. Charles Crocker, big in body, big in heart, big in ideas and big in execution. He is a typical American, "Go ahead" is his motto, "Never say die," is the principle upon which he works; an old 49'er, he went to California with an ox team, at a time when people would have deemed him insane to have talked of building a railroad over the mountains, he fought his way against flood and fire; he couldn't be drowned and he wouldn't be burned, he fought to the top every time. From contractor on the road he became an official, through every grade he passed, and is now the First Vice President of this grand line, which, had it not been for his energy, determination and toil, would never have extended beyond the Humbolt river. "Charley" Crocker is a *pusher*—but it don't do for any one to push him.

I accepted my friend's offer and his goods; part of the consignment I obtained advances upon. For a better market we removed to Salt Lake City.

We did well. We did better.

And we have been continuing to do better and better and better.

I have increased in size, property and family.

My wife, ditto, ditto, ditto; her increase in value to me has long since been beyond computation.

I was looking for my Luck, and found *HER*.

Finding *HER*, I found my *LUCK*.

Reader, Good Luck to you,

HANS LYKKEJÆGER.